A TRIP OF LOVE

KINNERA VENKAT

Made with ♥ on the Notion Press Platform
www.notionpress.com

To all the souls who believe in the magic of fate, the power of love, and the beauty of unexpected journeys.

With heartfelt gratitude to parents and family, whose love and sacrifices remain unmatched.

A sincere thank you to my loving husband, Mr. Venkatesh, for helping me find my way out of the darkness and for being the driving force behind my dreams. Your constant support and motivation mean the world to me. Love you!

Contents

Foreword

Every story has a heartbeat, and this one beats with love, hope, and the unexpected paths life often takes us on. In the pages that follow, you will find that love is not just a destination but a journey — one filled with small moments, quiet revelations, and the power of connection. As you read, may you be reminded that sometimes, the most beautiful things happen when we least expect them. It is a privilege to share this story, and I hope it brings you as much joy and reflection as it did for me in telling it.

— [Kinnera Venkat]

Preface

This story is a reflection of how life's unexpected turns can lead to the most beautiful destinations. Love is not just about grand gestures; it's about small moments, unspoken words, and the feeling of home in another person. I hope this novel touches your heart as much as it touched mine while writing it.

Acknowledgements

I would like to express my deepest gratitude to my husband for his constant support and encouragement throughout this journey. A special thank you to my mother and sisters for their unwavering belief in me, which kept me going. I also want to honor my late father, whose belief in me continues to inspire me every day. This book wouldn't have been possible without their love, faith, and encouragement.

— Kinnera Venkat]

Prologue

Life has a way of bringing together the most unexpected people at the most unexpected times. A single moment, a single decision, can alter the course of one's destiny. This is the story of Karthik and Krithi, two strangers brought together by fate, bound by an unspoken connection, and tested by time and distance.

ONE

A TRIP OF LOVE

A Journey of Heartfelt Moments

Karthik was standing at the top of a hill in Araku Valley, feeling the cool breeze on his face. Despite the chilly weather, he was thirsty, so he took out his water bottle and drank some water. As he was about to close the cap of the bottle, his eyes caught sight of something unexpected. A little girl, no older than five or six, was running toward the edge of the hill, heading straight for a dangerous area where the slope was steep and the drop was sheer. One wrong step, and she could fall from the height.

Without thinking, Karthik reacted instantly. He ran as fast as he could, his heart racing with concern. As he reached the girl, he grabbed her just in time, pulling her away from the edge of the hill and into his arms. His breath was heavy, but he felt a wave of relief wash over him as he held her safely.

Sitaara's parents, who had been walking nearby, had noticed the situation unfolding and immediately rushed toward them, leaving their belongings behind in their hurry. Sarath, the girl's father, looked visibly shaken but relieved when he saw his daughter in Karthik's arms. He quickly knelt down in front of Karthik, tears welling up in his eyes, and hugged Sitaara tightly as if he never wanted to let her go.

"Thank you. Thank you so much!" Sarath said, his voice full of emotion. "She is our world. You've saved her life. You're like a god to us. We will never forget what you did today. Please, stay in touch with us. Give us your contact information so we can thank you properly."

Sitaara's mother, who had been standing nearby, nodded in agreement, visibly overwhelmed by the gratitude. Sarath looked at Karthik, his eyes filled with a deep appreciation. It was clear that this moment meant everything to them, and they were forever indebted to him for his quick thinking and courage.

Karthik, though humbled by their gratitude, smiled and reassured them that it was nothing. However, Sarath insisted, and the two exchanged phone numbers, ensuring they could stay in touch. This connection, born out of a life-saving act, would stay with them for years to come.

Karthik and Sarath exchanged their phone numbers and spoke for a while. After coming down from the hill, they went to a fine dining restaurant for dinner. Sarath again thanked Karthik, and Karthik felt overwhelmed by their gratitude.

"We'll stay in touch, bro. I like Seethu too. She feels like a niece to me. We'll meet again," Karthik said. "But I have to leave now. I'm catching a bus to Hyderabad tonight for a meeting tomorrow."

Before leaving, Karthik kissed Sitaara on the forehead and said, "Take care, Seethu." He then left to catch the bus to Hyderabad.

After a fun four-day trip, Karthik walks into the office with a deep sigh. His feet feel heavy as he walks to his desk, and the usual office noise seems distant. He pulls out his chair, and the squeak echoes in the quiet room. Sitting down, he rubs his eyes for a moment, still feeling the relaxation from his break, but soon, tiredness takes over. He hovers his hands over the keyboard for a second before turning on his computer, watching the screen light up with a sense of both hesitation and duty. The stack of unread emails and tasks waiting for him makes him wish he could go back to the freedom of his trip, but he prepares himself to get back to work.

Karthik was checking his emails, which were sent by his manager and other company-related emails. He quickly replied to the urgent ones and looked through the rest to find work based on the emails. Meanwhile, his friend Prasad came over and asked, "Hey man, how was your trip? Let's go have a coffee."

Karthik and Prasad went for coffee. While filling their cups, Karthik said, "It was wonderful, machi. I feel so relaxed from this toxic work. That's why I'm having trouble concentrating on work now. My mind is still in Araku Valley with that family I met."

"Stop, stop! What family, bro? Did you meet a girlfriend there?" Prasad asked, laughing.

"No machi, the family with the little baby girl," Karthik replied, telling Prasad the whole story.

"Wow, that's awesome, man! They treated you like family? Did they have a girl for me to marry?" Prasad asked, laughing, since he was eagerly waiting for his bride but no matches had been found for him.

Karthik smiled and said, "Yes, Sarath bro has a sister, but she's getting married in two months. They asked me to come to the wedding and spend time with the whole family. They want to introduce me to their family and relatives."

Prasad grinned and asked, "In that case, I'll join you too, bro."

Karthik laughed and said, "Hey, uninvited fellow! I'm new to the family too, so don't get too crazy about it."

Suddenly, they saw their company director arriving. They quickly threw their cups into the trash and rushed back to their desks to get to work.

By the time Karthik finished his work, it was 9 PM. He packed his bag and went home. After freshening up, he asked his mother for food. She brought him his favorite dish, and the aroma filled the air. "Maa, I missed this food so much these days," Karthik said.

His mother smiled, rubbed his head, and asked, "How was your trip? We didn't get a chance to talk about it this morning."

Karthik told her about his trip, from his fun at the Vizag beach to meeting a nice family in Araku Valley. "Oh, that's nice! I'm so proud of you, my boy. I can imagine how happy that baby's mother must have felt. Well done, my boy," she said, kissing him on the forehead.

Karthik started eating, and his mother suddenly said, "You need to get married soon. I want you to have the company of a girl. I'm bored of just you and your younger brother."

Karthik, surprised, replied, "Maa, why this topic now? I need some time."

"How much time do you need, beta? Please get married. You can choose your girl. We trust you to make the right choice, and we won't complain," his mother said.

"Thanks for trusting me, Maa. Right now, I don't have anyone in my life, but let's see," Karthik replied.

"See soon, beta. I want to see our family grow," his mother said with a smile.

Both smiled, finished their dinner, and went to sleep.

Days passed with Karthik staying busy with work and family. A few days later, Sarath called Karthik and said, "My sister Devyani's wedding is fixed for March 23rd. Since it's February 20th now, we have less than a month. Please come with your family as soon as possible."

Karthik replied, "Okay, I'm happy to hear that! Convey my congratulations to Devyani. I'm not sure about my family, but I'll definitely come to meet you all. By the way, how is Bhabi and Seethu?"

Sarath replied, "All good. Seethu's craziness is increasing day by day. She's becoming uncontrollable with her actions."

Both laughed, and Karthik said, "Okay, bro, I'll see you soon. Good night."

Sarath said, "Good night, Karthik. Don't forget to come, even with your busy schedule."

Karthik replied, "No, bro, I'll definitely come. Devyani is like a sister to me, and this is also my family. Besides, I'll come to see Seethu too. I miss her."

Both smiled, said goodbye, and hung up.

The next day at the office, while working, Karthik called Prasad for a coffee break. They both went to the cafeteria, and Karthik said, "Sarath bro called me last night. His sister's wedding is on

March 23rd, and I have to go there a few days early to help with the wedding preparations. I'll be staying for five days or maybe a week, depending on the leave I get. I have to go because they consider me part of their family."

Prasad smiled and said, "That's great! Don't worry about your work here—we'll handle everything. You just enjoy the wedding vibes. And if you find someone beautiful there, let me know. I'll come and marry her!"

They both laughed, finished their coffee, and returned to work.

As Karthik got back to his desk, he thought, **"How am I going to survive all these days at Sarath bro's house, surrounded by so many relatives? Let's see... this might turn into the biggest adventure of my life—meeting and dealing with all these unknown people. Time to get ready for the ride!"** He rubbed his hair, adjusted his keyboard and mouse, and got back to work.

On the other hand, Devyani's wedding was approaching quickly. Sarath and his wife, Radhika, were managing all the wedding arrangements since their parents were old. Both of them were busy with wedding tasks as well as their personal work.

Devyani was caught up in the wedding excitement—shopping, making endless phone calls with her fiancé and in-laws, and planning for the big day.

As the days passed, Sarath went to Radhika's home to invite her parents and sister, Krithi. They assured him they would come around the wedding time, but Krithi would arrive three days earlier. She and Devyani were best friends, and they had a lot of preparations—and gossip—to catch up on before the wedding.

Radhika's mother chuckled and said, "Alright, dear. But you seem very busy."

"Yes, Mom. I still have many wedding invitations to distribute, and I'm the only one doing it for now. My brother will be here in two days, so we'll divide the work."

Her mother looked puzzled. "Your brother? As far as I know, you don't have a brother."

Sarath smiled. "Karthik! The guy who saved Seethu from danger when we went to Araku."

"Oh, that young man! He seems like a really nice person. I'd love to meet him and thank him again."

Sarath laughed and said, "I'll tell him, Aunty. And please remind Krithi to come early, or else Devyani will start scolding her!"

Everyone laughed, and Sarath waved goodbye, saying, "Take care!"

As the days passed, Devyani's wedding was getting closer. Karthik had to pack his bags and leave for Vizag from Hyderabad. After packing, he said goodbye to his mother and stepped into Prasad's car.

Prasad waved at Karthik's mother and said, "Bye, Aunty! Don't worry, Karthik will be back in a few days. In the meantime, If You need anything just call me—I'll fly over immediately but Please note down you should cook chicken for me before I come!"

Everyone laughed at Prasad's joke.

"Aunty, if you need anything, just call me. I'm always available, so don't hesitate to ask," Prasad again added.

Karthik's mother smiled and said, "Okay, okay! Now go, it's time for your train."

"Bye, Mom!" Karthik said, giving her a final wave.

"Bye, Aunty! Take care!" Prasad added as they drove off in his red Swift car.

When they reached the railway station, Karthik once again explained his work responsibilities to Prasad.

Prasad interrupted, "Hey, stop worrying, man! Just go and enjoy the wedding. We'll handle everything here. Don't think too much. Take care! Bye!"

With a smile, Karthik stepped onto the train, found his seat—number 47 in B2—and finally settled in. He turned on some music on his phone and connected his *boAt* AirPods, enjoying his playlist.

Meanwhile, a middle-aged woman approached him and asked, "Beta, can you please take my seat and give me yours? I can't climb up. I had surgery a month ago, and it's difficult for me."

Karthik immediately agreed and switched to the upper berth. He lay down and continued listening to music when he suddenly remembered he needed to inform Sarath about his departure.

He quickly dialed Sarath's number.

"Bro, I'm on my way! Please pick me up tomorrow at Vizag railway station," Karthik said.

Sarath replied cheerfully, "That's great! Seethu and I will come to pick you up—if she wakes up that early in the morning."

"Tell her that *Chachu* is coming tomorrow morning. Then she won't sleep at all, and neither will you!" Karthik laughed.

Sarath chuckled. "That's true! She'll keep asking me and *Bhabhi* all night, 'When will Karthi Chachu come?'"

They both laughed.

"Alright, bro! I'll call you once I step out of the station," Karthik said.

"Okay, Karthik! We'll be waiting for you. Take care," Sarath replied.

As the sun rose, its golden rays filled the train compartment. The noise around him woke Karthik up. He immediately checked his phone to track the train's location.

"Yes! It's almost at Vizag," he thought. "I have to get ready."

Karthik grabbed his luggage and mobiles, climbed down from the upper berth, and headed toward the washbasin to freshen up. He splashed water on his face, feeling the cold morning air. The sight of Vizag's beautiful scenery outside the train window made him smile.

He returned to his seat and sat down. Soon, a man selling beverages walked through the train, calling out, "Coffee! Coffee! Tea! Coffee! Who wants coffee?"

Karthik stopped him and said, "One coffee, please."

The vendor handed him a cup and said, "That'll be 20 rupees, sir."

Karthik paid him and said, "Thanks!"

The vendor smiled and continued moving down the aisle, repeating, "Coffee! Tea! Coffee! Tea!"

Karthik took a sip of his coffee, enjoying the refreshing taste while admiring the scenic beauty of Vizag as the train approached the station.

Finally, the train arrived at Vizag station. Karthik stepped out with his luggage and called Sarath.

"Bro, I'm here! I've reached Vizag and I'm standing outside the station," Karthik said.

Sarath answered, "Nice, man! I'm in the parking area. Coming towards you."

A few moments later, Sarath arrived. Karthik got into the car and greeted him, "Hi, bro! How are you? Where is Seethu? Didn't she come?"

He looked into the backseat, expecting to see Seethu, but instead, he saw another girl.

"No, Karthik, Seethu is still sleeping. I just picked up Radhika's sister, Krithi," Sarath said, pointing to the girl in the backseat. "Krithi, this is Karthik, my brother—the one who saved our Seethu that day in Vizag."

Krithi smiled and said, "Hi! And thanks for saving our little world, Seethu."

Karthik smiled back and said my pleasure. "Hey, Krithi! *Bhabhi* is such a nice lady, I'm sure you are too."

Krithi laughed, and Karthik asked, "What do you do, Krithi?"

Sarath answered, "Both Radhika and Krithi are great people. Krithi loves Seethu a lot. She works as a Financial Analyst in Bengaluru."

"Oh, a Financial Analyst? That's nice! I was very poor in Mathematics," Karthik joked.

Everyone laughed, and Krithi said, "Hey Karthik, accounts is not just about math! It's about managing money efficiently for work and businesses. And by the way, math is everywhere in life."

"Of course, that's why I try my best to stay far away from it!" Karthik said, making everyone laugh again.

As they continued chatting, they reached Sarath's home.

Karthik, Sarath, and Krithi stepped out of the car, collecting their luggage. Just then, Radhika and Seethu came out to greet them.

Seethu ran excitedly towards Karthik and hugged him. "Thanks for coming, Chachu!" she said happily.

Radhika hugged Krithi took Krithi's bag and asked Krithi and Karthik, "How are you, Guys? Welcome home!"

"I'm great, *Bhabhi*! How about you?" Karthik replied.

"I'm busy with Seethu and all the wedding preparations. You know how hectic weddings can be!" she said with a smile. "Come inside, take a shower, and then we'll have breakfast."

Seethu then ran to Krithi, hugged her tightly, and said, "I missed you, Chachi!"

"I missed you too, Seethu *Dear*!" Krithi replied warmly.

They all went inside. Radhika turned to Krithi and said, "You freshen up in our bedroom." Then she looked at Sarath, "Show Karthik his room. Meanwhile, I'll prepare breakfast for us."

Just then, Sarath's parents came out.

Sarath introduced Karthik to them, and Karthik immediately moved forward to take their blessings.

They placed their hands on his head and said, "We are very grateful to you, *beta*. Now go freshen up, and then we will all have breakfast together before starting the wedding work."

Uncle asked Krithi how are you beti?, Krithi also stepped forward to take blessings from her in-laws, saying, "I'm good, Aunty and Uncle."

Everyone then went to their rooms to freshen up.

After freshening up, they all gathered at the dining table. Radhika brought breakfast and placed it on the table, while Krithi helped by serving plates and water.

The house was filled with warmth, laughter, and the excitement of the upcoming wedding.

Later, Karthik and Sarath went out to buy wedding decorative items, while Krithi and Devyani went out to buy cosmetics. The rest of the group stayed at home and focused on their tasks related to the wedding, making phone calls to friends and relatives. By the end of the day, everyone returned home and sat down after dinner. They began talking about plans to go out after the wedding, including a devotional trip and Devyani's honeymoon trip, which would include Karthik and the family. Everyone was excited about the idea.

As their conversation continued, they enjoyed a delicious dessert made by Krithi. Everyone praised her for the taste, but Karthik hesitated to say more, unsure of what was going on inside him. Eventually, everyone became sleepy, and the conversation came to an end.

For the first three days after the wedding, they planned a family trip, starting with a visit to the famous Ayodhya Ram Mandir, followed by visits to nearby temples and Agra. The trip was planned to go from Ayodhya to Agra for the family, and after three or four days, Devyani and her husband could decide to disperse as they wished. They would then move on to Simla for their honeymoon.

Krithi and Devyani were taking all the dessert cups and glasses to the kitchen when Karthik said, "I'll help you guys. I'm coming!" Later, Krithi, Devyani, and Karthik headed to the kitchen. Devyani walked ahead, with Karthik catching up to Krithi. He turned to her and said, "Krithi, that was a nice dessert. I really liked it. I've never had something like that before. Thank you so much! Would you make it again for me, whenever you can?"

Krithi smiled and replied, "Is it? Maybe you're overestimating my cooking skills. It turned out well this time, but I'm not sure it'll be the same next time. But anyway, I'll make it for you."

"Thank you, Krithi," Karthik said. They put the bowls and glasses in the kitchen sink, and as they did, they looked at each other and laughed. Both said, "Good night!" and went to their rooms.

The next morning, the decorative items and flowers arrived by van, along with a few workers. Everyone started working, with Karthik supervising the decoration on a sunny day. By around 12 PM, the workers were laboring under the hot sun, so Radhika sent juices for everyone, along with Krithi.

Krithi went around handing out the drinks and, when she reached Karthik, he smiled and said, "I'm not working and I'm not tired, Krithi. Why are you giving me juice?"

She smiled back and said, "I can see you're working hard, Karthik. I can see the sweat on your face, from your head to your cheeks."

Karthik accepted the juice, and as Krithi walked away, he thought, *Is she really observing me that much?* He smiled to himself. Meanwhile, Krithi, while heading back, also felt something different when talking to him. Her heart filled with joy every time they spoke. She couldn't help but notice the minor changes in herself.

Meanwhile, Sharath went out to invite some guests. Radhika called Karthik to have lunch several times, but Karthik couldn't come because he was busy helping the workers and had to go out to pick up more items. He finally returned around 4 PM, after giving all the decoration items to the workers. Feeling tired, he sat down outside the door while everyone was busy with their own work.

Krithi noticed him and walked over, asking, "Did you have lunch?"

"No," Karthik replied. "I had to go out, so I just got back. I'm really hungry. Is there anything left to eat?"

Krithi looked concerned and said, "Oh no, I think there's nothing left. Everyone had lunch. Just wait, I'll go check the kitchen."

She went into the kitchen and checked one by one: the rice was empty, the curry was finished... nothing was left to eat. "What should I do?" she said to herself. Then, she opened the fridge and found juices, fruits, and sweets. First, she poured juice into a glass and went outside to give it to Karthik.

"Sorry, Karthik. There's nothing left, just fruits, sweets, and juices. Can I cut the fruits for you? Then I'll make something else for you in the meantime."

Karthik smiled and replied, "No, thanks for the juice. I'll go out to buy some other items and eat something there."

He stood up from the sofa and started to walk, but then he stopped and called out to Krithi, saying, "Don't tell Radhika that I didn't have lunch. She might feel bad."

"Okay, but are you really okay?" Krithi asked, feeling bad for not feeding him.

"I'm absolutely fine, dear," Karthik replied, with a smile. "Why are you worrying so much? It's okay. Sometimes, I'm fine even without lunch." He smiled again and added, "How could I stay dull when my girl gave me juice with so much warmth?"

As soon as he said "my girl," he cursed himself for the slip of the tongue. Krithi looked at him, a bit confused, and asked, "What did you say?"

With a small smile and a slight confusion, Karthik quickly cursed himself again and ran off, leaving Krithi puzzled but smiling.

Is he attracting towards me? He is not understanding but he is nice guys, Krithi said to herself smiled and back to her work.

After a while, Krithi's father and mother arrived, and everyone at home welcomed them. Karthik stood beside them with a smile. Sarath introduced Karthik to his in-laws, explaining that Karthik was the one who had saved Sitaara. Then, Karthik went to take their blessings. "Ayushman Bhava," Krithi's mother said as she blessed him, followed by her father. "Thank you so much, Karthik. We are really grateful to you. 'Thanks' isn't enough," Krithi's parents said. Karthik responded, "I'm equally thankful to your family for accepting me. Especially Seethu, by lifting her up to kiss her—she is the princess of my life."

Devyani then asked, "By the way, is there a queen in your life, bro?" Everyone sat on the sofas as Radhika's parents had just arrived and were looking at Karthik, waiting for his answer. Krithi was excited to hear it. Karthik thought to himself, "I don't know if she'll be in my life. I don't know what feelings I have for her, but I have a girl in mind, though I haven't proposed yet." Finally, Karthik said, "Currently, no one is there. My mother has given me permission to find a girl, and I'm grateful for the trust she has in me."

Radhika then asked, "So, we will search for her, Karthik. Is that okay with you?" Karthik thought to himself, "You don't need to search; she might be right beside you, Bhabi." He responded, "Of course, but not right now. I need to settle down a bit more."

"That's a good idea, Karthik. We should settle first before a lady enters our life. We need to take care of everything for her and for ourselves," Sarath said.

Everyone enjoyed their tea, which the maid had served, and the conversation shifted to wedding plans. After they finished their tea, Karthik and Sarath took permission from the family and left for their work.

After their conversation ended, everyone got back to their work. Tomorrow night is Devyani's wedding, and she feels a mix of emotions – fear, anxiety, and happiness – as she's about to start a new chapter in her life with Rajiv, the person she loves. Rajiv called Devyani to talk, but she hesitated. Though she's happy, she felt anxious inside, so she told him that her feelings were hard to explain and that they would talk later.

Then Rajiv texted Krithi, saying that Devyani was worried. He asked her to give Devyani some strength, as she might feel like she's leaving her family tomorrow to be with him. Krithi replied, "Don't worry, Bhayya. I'll take care of her. You enjoy your wedding." Then, she added jokingly, "By the way, when is your bachelor party?"

Rajiv chuckled and replied, "It's tonight, Krithi. Would you join us with my wife?"

Krithi laughed and said, "Oh, you're planning to meet your wife? Am I supposed to be the mediator, bro? No, bro, I don't want to take your time. Enjoy your party with your friends, and here we'll enjoy the mehendi party with a bit of gossip." Both of them chuckled before hanging up.

After the call, Krithi went to check on Devyani in her room. On her way, Krithi's mother called. "I'll talk to you later, mom. I want to talk to Devyani now," Krithi said.

Her mother replied, "That's why I'm calling you, baby. Give Devyani this juice; she's feeling weak with all the wedding preparations."

Krithi took the juice from her mother and went to Devyani's room. She knocked on the door. "Hey, why are you knocking? Just come in!" Devyani called out.

Krithi smiled and said, "You're the bride now, so I thought you might have some secret phone calls. I wanted to ask for permission before entering." She handed Devyani the juice. "By the way, you're glowing more and more every day. You're really excited to see my brother and spend time with him, right?"

Krithi chuckled.

"Yes, that's partly true," Devyani replied. "I'm so excited to be with Rajiv, but I'm also going to miss my family – my mom, dad, Sarath, and Bhabi. Especially Seethu. I'll miss the cheerful days at home. I'm also nervous about moving to a new family. I don't know how they'll welcome me, or how I'll adjust to their ways. All these thoughts are mixed up in my mind, and I feel something I can't explain. I'm glad you came at the right time to talk to me."

"No worries, dear. I'm here for you," Krithi reassured her. "Now, drink the juice, and then we need to go for the mehendi. By the way, are your friends coming tonight?"

"Yes, they'll be here in about two hours," Devyani replied. "I've already informed Sarath to take care of their accommodation and needs. They'll come straight to the mehendi function after they freshen up at the hotel."

Mehandi function going to start sharath and Karthik took the item which they need for Mehandhi function and they are going back it is a ladies function. Devyani, Krithi, Radhika, Devyani's friends and other ladies got ready to attend the function and enjoy with latest music songs and dances. While moving out from home Karthik Asked krithi I wanted to join your function could you please help me in this? No it's a ladies function man no men is allowed. It won't happen. It will be happen when you and Devyani is said ok. Just say ok please.. Devyani said her friends are very beautiful I'll select one of them please Krithi, Karthik teased her. O you need to select one? For that I have to help you? What is this Karthik she smiled and said. Yes you have to help me please, hey why you asking that many times I already told you that this is a ladies function no men presence we don't need. Needddd I got it I'll come as a photo grapgher assistant there Karthik said. Karthik don't do this we need privacy. Ok bye don't come Krithi said and went to the mehandi function stage to check is there everthing is fine or not.

Everything was set for the function. All the ladies had arrived, and the DJ started playing music. Some girls sat down to design mehendi on each other's hands, while others danced to the music. Meanwhile, Karthik entered without permission and started recording the dance on his phone. Krithi was dancing in a peacock style. "Wow, she's a great dancer. She looks gorgeous in this dress," Karthik thought to himself.

He then said to himself, "Maybe I'm falling in love with her more and more each day. I need to be careful. But if she comes into my life, I'll be the happiest person in the world. Maybe she's the right one for me. I'll wait and then propose to her. I don't want to miss her. She's such a wonderful girl."

Karthik stopped the video as Krithi finished dancing and went to get mehendi done on her hands. He grabbed a mini camera to take some pictures and said to Krithi, "Please pose!" He clicked a photo of her as she was getting mehendi applied by another girl. She was wearing a light pink ghagra and had loose hair, looking stunning.

Surprised, Krithi asked, "Hey Karthik, why are you here? I told you not to come."

"Sorry, dear, I came for work," Karthik replied, showing her the camera. Krithi didn't say anything else, just waved him aside and said, "Go ahead with your work."

Karthik then went to Devyani and her friends, taking pictures. Without realizing it, Karthik ended up taking more photos of Krithi than of Devyani.

Finally, the wedding day arrived. Everyone was getting ready for the ceremony, and Devyani was dressed in her bridal attire. She looked like a goddess, with a radiant face and a sparkling smile. She was the happiest girl in the world, eagerly waiting to see Rajiv in his groom's attire.

Krithi walked in and said, **"The groom's family has arrived! He looks even better than you, my dear!"** teasing Devyani. Devyani smiled, feeling both happy and a little nervous as time was moving fast, bringing her closer to a new life.

Relatives came to see Devyani and admired her beauty, saying, "**You look like a Radiant Rose.**" Everyone praised her bridal look, and she smiled, thanking them all.

Meanwhile, Rajiv was eager to see Devyani after hearing so many compliments about her beauty. His excitement grew, but as per tradition, they were not allowed to see each other until after the **Cumin-Jaggery Bonding Ritual.** Respecting the custom, Rajiv decided to wait and see her for the first time at the **Mandap Seating.**

Sarath was busy welcoming and greeting guests, while Radhika helped the priest with the pooja and wedding preparations. Devyani's friends and relatives were busy taking pictures of their outfits. The aunties were gossiping, the uncles were looking around the wedding hall and decorations, and everyone was chatting with each other.

In the middle of all this, Karthik was looking for Krithi, excited to see how she had dressed for the occasion. He was slowly falling in love with her and loved being around her. Holding a camera, he walked around the wedding hall, hoping to capture her beauty.

It was time for the bride's arrival for the **Pre-Wedding Blessing Ritual**, and Devyani was on her way. Radhika, Krithi, and other ladies held her hands and walked beside her, guiding her to the **mandapam**. Everyone in the audience stared at her in awe—she looked stunning.

She sat on the **wedding seat**, and the priest began explaining the wedding rituals to her. The groom's mother and sister came to the **mandapam**, offering her sarees and ornaments for the marriage while giving her their blessings.

Devyani then got up to change into the saree given by Rajiv's mother, which she was supposed to wear for the wedding ceremony. After she left, Rajiv took her place and continued performing the rituals as instructed by the priest before the wedding ceremony officially began.

Devyani's parents gave Rajiv new clothes and other necessary items. He then got ready, wearing the traditional dhoti. Once both were ready, the priest asked them to sit, and he began guiding the couple through the rituals while chanting mantras, following the traditional wedding customs.

After Rajiv tied the sacred knot with Devyani, everyone in the crowd showered them with blessings, holy rice, and flowers. Finally, the wedding was complete. Everyone blessed them and took photos with the newlyweds.

During the family photo session, Sarath called Karthik to join in. Karthik's eyes filled with happy tears, feeling touched by how they accepted him as part of the family.

After the blessings, photos, and gifts, Devyani and Rajiv were heading to Rajiv's home to complete the formalities. Before leaving, Devyani took blessings from her parents, Sarath and Radhika, and Radhika's parents. She looked at Karthik and said, "You're the most precious brother God has given me. Thank you so much for being a part of our lives." Karthik smiled and I'm really bleesed to have you all in my life. Take care dear.

Devyani then went to Seethu who stood beside Krithi and said, "Bye, Seethu. Don't make too much noise, and don't irritate your mom, okay?" Seethu smiled and nodded, then Devyani hugged Krithi and said, "Thanks for everything."

Everyone there got emotional as Devyani and Rajiv left in the car. Sarath and the family waved goodbye, feeling heavy-hearted, missing her already.

After completing the family rituals at Rajiv's home, Rajiv, Devyani, and Rajiv's parents returned to Devyani's house, as they had planned a trip before the wedding. Both families were going to start their journey by train. Sarath's mother instructed Radhika and Devyani to pack snacks and dinner for the night.

Radhika and Devyani were busy packing, and Krithi also came to help. Meanwhile, all the men were enjoying tea and chatting in the living room. Once everything was packed, they loaded their luggage into the cars. Sarath's friends also came to drop them off at the railway station.

While Krithi was carrying a heavy bag, Karthik took it from her to help and placed it in the car. "Thanks," she said quietly. Karthik smiled slightly.

Everyone got into the cars and headed to the railway station, where they searched for their train, **Bhogi B5**. They found it and boarded the train, settling their luggage. After everything was arranged, they sat down and started chatting.

Meanwhile, Prasad called Karthik, saying, "Hey man, how are you? You've forgotten about us and the company!" He chuckled.

"I'm doing great, man. How about you?" Karthik replied.

"Everything's good here. The manager asked when you'll be coming back, and I need a file that's in your system. Can you tell me the name of the file?"

"Just search for it using office credentials. You'll find it," Karthik replied.

"Okay, bro. When will you be back?"

"I'm going to Ayodhya and Agra with Sarath's family. Once we're back, I'll come home the same day."

"Okay, Karthik. Bye."

"Bye," Karthik said, ending the call.

Sarath asked, "Karthik, is everything okay?"

"Yes, bro. No issues. Just a friend asked about a file I have," Karthik replied.

"Alright, let's have dinner," Sarath said.

Both of them went to the seats occupied by the elders, and everyone began eating rotis for dinner. Everyone ate in their own way, but Seethu kept troubling Radhika to eat. Karthik called Seethu over, telling her some kids' stories, and fed her. Krithi watched him with a positive opinion. **"How good and simple he is... he seems very caring,"** she thought to herself.

After dinner, Sarath instructed everyone that the younger ones should settle in the upper berths, while the senior citizens would occupy the lower berths. Everyone went to their assigned places as Sarath had instructed.

Karthik settled on side upper berth and Krithi settled upperberth of 3seats and connected her bluettoth and listening songs through her airpods. Karthik Messaged her.

Karthik: Hi

Krithi: Hi

Karthik: I'm bored. Can you keep me company through chat?

Krithi: Yeah, it's okay. I'm listening to music now.

Karthik: Okay... Which songs?

Krithi: All melody songs which are in my play list .

Karthik: What else? Tell me about yourself.

Krithi: Is this an interview?

Karthik: No, just wanna know.

Krithi: I'm in my final semester of MBA. I want to go abroad and do my MS there.

Karthik: What?

Krithi: Why?

Karthik: You want to settle abroad?

Krithi: Not really, but I can't say no either. Why?

Karthik: India is better than other countries.

Krithi: Hey, where is this going? Are you against settling abroad?

Karthik: No, nothing like that. I just don't want to settle abroad for myself.

Krithi: Why?

Karthik: I don't know. I just want to stay here. That's all.

Krithi: Excuse me, are you trying to stop me? That's why you're explaining about staying here.

Karthik: No, Krithi. I'm just saying. So, you want to do your MS and come back?

Krithi: Maybe. If everything goes well, I'll stay a few years there.

Karthik: Oh, that's okay. What else, Krithi tell me more about you.

Krithi: So, what about you?

Karthik: I'm a software engineer. My work is stressful, so I came to Araku to refresh. That's when I met Sarath and now I'm here with all of you.

Krithi: Okay. Then

Karthik: Do you have a boyfriend?

Krithi: I don't think much about it. I'll live my life. I'll marry the person chosen by my dad and family. I don't want to struggle with emotions. I don't want to mess it up.

Karthik: Why are you talking weird about boyfriends? Any breakup stories?

Krithi: No, Karthik, not at all. I don't want to think about such things.

Karthik: Okay, sorry. Even I don't have any girl in my life until I met your family.

Krithi: Until I met your family? But now? Is there anyone? Did you set any girl in this marriage?

Karthik: Maybe... May not be... Might be...

Krithi: Hey, just tell me. I won't tell anyone at home.

Karthik: No, Krithi. I'll tell you for sure once the time comes.

Karthik: By the way, what's your opinion about me? Am I a good person?

Krithi: If you ask directly like this, what can I say?

Karthik: Just tell me casually.

Krithi: You're a good person, good looking, and a good human being. All our family likes you.

Karthik: Oh, thanks. What about you? Did you like me?

Krithi: ??

Karthik: I mean, did you like my personality and behavior?

Krithi: Yes, of course. But without knowing you, how can I say you're a good person?

Karthik: Thanks for coming into my life, Krithi. I mean, thanks for chatting with me. You can sleep now. Good night, sweet dreams!

Krithi: Okay, Karthik. Good night.

(Krithi covered her head with a white bedsheet. Karthik looked at her once, then put his phone on silent and went to sleep.)

The next morning, sunrays were hitting the rain-soaked windows of the train. Everyone woke up, freshened up with brushing their teeth and face washes, and then sat together. Soon, coffee was served, and everyone drank it. Sarath's mother was worried about breakfast and lunch because they wouldn't reach their destination until evening. She wondered how they would manage food in the train. Sarath reassured her, saying, "Don't worry, Maa, we can order food from Zomato."

They all continued to talk, sharing previous experiences. Meanwhile, Sarath and Radhika's father ordered breakfast for everyone. Seethu and Krithi sat on the side berth, enjoying the view of nature through the windows. As soon as the train reached the next station, all the breakfast orders were delivered.

Karthik brought a plate of dosas for Krithi and himself. She thanked him, and Radhika called Seethu to come and eat the idlis. Seethu ran over to her mother, while Krithi started eating. Karthik then asked her, "Can I sit here?" Krithi smiled and said, "Hey, why not? Please sit, let's have breakfast together."

As they ate, Karthik said, "Thank you for last night." Krithi replied, "Why are you thanking me? We just had a small chat." Karthik responded, "Yes, but you gave me your time."

Krithi smiled and said, "Karthik, I'm not a politician or a celebrity, I'm just one of your family members." Karthik smiled back and thanked her again. Krithi smiled and went to wash her hands. Karthik followed her.

Once they reached the washbasin, Karthik called out to Krithi, "Can I tell you something?"

"Yes, Karthik, what is it?" Krithi asked.

But Karthik just smiled and returned to his seat. "What happened to him?" Krithi thought to herself. She returned to her seat, sat down, and started reading a book titled *All Rights Reserved For You*. After a while, Seethu came to sit beside her. Krithi closed the book and started enjoying the view of nature once again.

Meanwhile, Devyani came to Krithi, sat next to her, and started talking. "What are you doing, Krithi? Isn't it boring with all the elders?" Krithi smiled and replied, "Of course! That's why I enjoy my own way—reading sometimes, talking with everyone sometimes, and just watching outside sometimes."

Dveyani said, "Give company to Karthik. He's sitting alone over there." She pointed to Karthik's seat.

Krithi, can I ask you something?" Devyani asked. "Sure," Krithi replied.

"Is Karthik talking to you?" Devyani asked.

"Yes, we chatted for a few minutes yesterday. Why?" Krithi asked.

"What did he say?" Devyani inquired.

"He asked about my studies, if I have a boyfriend, and bla bla bla... and finally, he said thanks. I don't know why he said that," Krithi explained. "He's behaving a little differently."

"Differently how?" Devyani asked.

"Maybe he's attracted to me, I thought, because of his actions and the way he talks. But it's not in a bad way. He's a good guy."

"Oh, is he good?" Devyani chuckled.

"Good means good, nothing else!" Krithi laughed.

"Okay then. I want to show you something. We got the raw wedding photos. Come, I'll show you," Devyani said.

Krithi followed her to Rajiv's laptop. "These are the photos we took ourselves at the mini ceremonies at home," Devyani explained. "Sarath bro asked Karthik to take the photos because he's a good photographer."

"Did you notice? Your photos are more than mine," Devyani said.

"Maybe he's interested in you, Krithi," Devyani teased. "Just observe him. He's a good guy. I'll help my brother if he tells me about it."

"He's really nice. I've talked to his mother several times too, and she's so sweet," Devyani added, continuing to tease Krithi.

"Stop it, Devyani!" Krithi said, laughing. "I have to finish my MS first. After that, I'll think about my partner. Until then, no looking at anyone," Krithi said with a smile.

After lunch, Krithi, Devyani, Rajiv, and Karthik sat together and started talking. Rajiv asked Karthik, "Tell us about yourself, Karthik. What do you do?"

Karthik replied, "I'm a senior software engineer. I'm working on a big project and aiming for a promotion. Also sometimes I've been traveling alone for a while."

"All alone, bro?" Devyani asked.

"I wish I could travel with someone, but I'm hoping someone special will come into my life," Karthik said.

"Who is she? Can you show us her photo? What is she studying?" Rajiv asked.

Karthik responded, "I can't show her photo, but she is currently studying. She plans to complete her MS in the US."

"Is she already in the US?" Devyani asked.

"No, she plans to go there," Karthik said.

Devany and Krithi exchanged looks, like they had figured something out. "Oh, Krithi is also planning to go to the US! Maybe they'll meet there!" Devyani said to Karthik.

Karthik smiled, and Krithi jokingly cursed Devyani.

"Bro, tell us your love story!" Devyani said.

"My love story hasn't started yet. I haven't proposed to her yet. It's one-sided love, but I hope to tell her soon," Karthik explained.

"We're all waiting for that moment, bro! I want to see your proposal in person!" Devyani chuckled.

Krithi playfully slapped her shoulder and said, "Stop it, Devyani."

"So Krithi, maybe you both will stay in the US and spend time together? Maybe even live in the same house?" Rajiv said.

Krithi gave him an artificial smile and said, "Yes, if Karthik says okay, we can stay together."

Karthik hesitated for a few seconds and then replied, "Yes, we'll stay together... with my loved one."

"With who?" Devyani asked.

"With me," Karthik said. "I mean, with my loved one."

Karthik quickly excused himself and walked toward the door to avoid the topic. Devyani followed him.

"What's going on, bro? I can tell something's going on with your love life," Devyani teased.

Karthik whispered, "Shh... I know you understand, but don't tell anyone until I tell her. Devyani smiled and karthik said, Thanks for the support."

Both Devyani and Karthik returned to their seats, while Krithi felt nervous, confused, happy, and a bit tensed. Even though Karthik hadn't proposed yet, she realized that the girl he liked was actually her.

Rajiv asked, "What about you, Krithi?"

"I have to go to the US first. I'll focus on my education and job there," Krithi replied.

"What about a boyfriend or love?" Devyani asked.

"No, nothing like that until I finish my MS. I don't want to get distracted. I'll focus on my studies and think about love later," Krithi said.

"What kind of guy do you want?" Devyani asked.

"Someone with a good personality, good-looking, well-settled, who respects elders, and is understanding... Oh, there's a long list!" Krithi said.

Devayani teased, "I know a guy who fits all those qualities. Can I talk to him?"

Krithi playfully hit her on the shoulder and said, "Stop it!"

Everyone laughed.

The train was nearing the destination, so they all started picking up their luggage to get off.

After getting off the train, everyone went to the hotel they had booked for the night. The next day, they were going to visit Ayodhya for the darshan of Lord Rama. They went to their rooms, freshened up, and then came out for dinner. After having their meal, they were all tired from the journey and knew they had to wake up early to go to the temple. So, they all went to sleep.

The next day, they had their darshan at the temple and then went to visit another place. Once reached to the next temple, they got out of the hired car. Karthik was the last one to get out and noticed a Wallet that had fallen under the seat. He picked it up and opened it to see who it belonged to. Inside, he found a photo of a small baby boy. Karthik didn't know whose purse it was, so he asked everyone in the group if they recognized the Wallet.

Krithi's father checked his pocket but didn't find anything missing. He then said, "Karthik, it's mine."

"Oh, okay, Uncle! Here you go, take care of it," Karthik said.

"Thank you, Beta. This is precious to me," Krithi's father said.

Then, they all walked toward the temple. On the way, Karthik asked, "Uncle, can I ask you something?"

"Yes, Karthik," Krithi's father replied.

"Who is the baby boy in your wallet?" Karthik asked.

Krithi's father paused for a moment and said, "That's my son."

"Do you have a son, Uncle? Where is he?" Karthik asked.

"It's a long story, Karthik. We'll talk about it later," Krithi's father replied.

Their conversation ended, and they went into the temple to complete their darshan. But Karthik was still confused about the baby in the photo. After they returned to the vehicle, Krithi's father started to tell the story, as Karthik had kept asking about it.

He began, "His name is Virat. We used to visit the Jagannatha temple every year. But when our son was 4 years old, we lost him in the crowd. We searched everywhere and even filed a police complaint, but we couldn't find him because the crowd was so huge. Every year, I go to the temple and check with the police. One day, the police told us that someone from the south had rescued him from a stampede. The couple who found him took him with them because he was crying so much. Since then, we've been visiting temples in the south, hoping that one day, a god or goddess will return our son. But we also understand that if we bring him back, those parents will be heartbroken because they've raised him for more than 30 years."

Krithi's father's eyes filled with tears as he remembered his son. Krithi continued, "My dad always told us that Virat had a unique talent. Even when he was very young, he could recognize the person who was in back of a camera(The person who is taking the photo). If he saw any photo, he would also tell us the name of another person in the photo—the person who was taking the picture.

Krithi's father continuing to tell for example, one day we went to the park. Myself, my wife, and Virat stood for a photo that was being taken by our friend, Ramana. Later, when Virat was able to talk, he told us, 'Ramana uncle is also there,' even though he was very small and could only speak in his childish way.

Another time, when we went to visit our relatives, Virat saw a photo of the couple and said, 'Dad is also there.' After hearing this several times, we realized that Virat had a unique talent."

Krithi added, "We were all amazed when we first heard about this."

"Wow, really?" Karthik exclaimed, impressed by this unique quality. At the same time, he remembered that one of his friend's brother, who works in forensics, has the same talent. His parents had adopted him. Karthik didn't say anything to Krithi's family, though, because he wasn't sure if there could be other people with the same talent. He thought to himself, *I should talk to Rama Aunty when I get back to Hyderabad. She's the one who adopted Virat.*

After completing all the temple visits, they were heading back to the hotel to go to Agra. It was nighttime after dinner when Karthik asked Krithi in a message if she had heard anything about their brother, Virat.

Krithi: I don't know him; I wasn't even born then. My parents used to tell me about him, so that's how I know.

Karthik: Oh, it's okay. So, what else, Krithi? After our Agra tour, I'll miss you all... especially YOU

Krithi: Especially me?? Why?

Karthik: "You told me you're going abroad, right? If you're in Vizag, I'll come to visit sometimes."

Krithi: "You can come to the USA too," she sent with a smile.

Karthik: "Me? Abroad? Let's see, if the moment calls for it, I'll definitely come there."

Krithi: "The moment calls for you? What do they say? You're talking very nicely and differently, Karthik. I like the way you speak."

Karthik: "Oh, thank you so much. I believe in living in the moment. Right now, I'm with you, and this moment is with you."

Krithi: "Ooh, okay. I see there's a poet within you. 'Believe, live'—nice line."

Karthik: "Thank you, dear. When will we meet again? After our Agra trip, I'll be heading back to Hyderabad, and you guys will go to Vizag."

Krithi: "Maybe when I'm flying. I'll come to Hyderabad for shopping before going to the USA, then we'll meet."

Karthik: "Oh, that's nice. You should meet my mom too. She's a wonderful person, just like you. She's my stress buster."

Krithi: "Yes, Karthik, I'll definitely come and meet your mom too."

Karthik: "Let me know a week before so I can take leave, and I'll come shopping with you so we can spend more time together."

Krithi: "Can you give me your manager's number? Who is your manager? He sent you on a trip, allowed time for marriage, and even gave you more leave? He seems so kind," Krithi chuckled.

Karthik: "Haha, I work as much as he wants, and then he gives me as many leaves as I need. Work first!"

Krithi: "Okay, Karthik. Mom's calling me to sleep. Good night!"

Karthik: "Good night, Krithi," he sent with a heart symbol.

Krithi smiled in her heart when she saw the heart emoji, locked her phone, and put it aside before going to sleep for the next day's visit to the Taj Mahal.

The next morning, everyone got ready and went to see the world wonder, the Taj Mahal. As they were walking through the Taj Mahal garden, Karthik took photos of everyone, especially Krithi. He wanted to take a photo with her, but he hesitated. He wanted to take a picture with her beside him as his soulmate, so he waited for the right moment.

Devyani and Rajiv were taking amazing photos, looking like the perfect couple. Karthik was still taking pictures of them and guiding them on the poses.

Krithi noticed that Karthik was standing under the sun and sweating. She walked over to him and called out, "Karthik."

He turned, and she handed him a water bottle.

He took the bottle, smiled, drank, and then gave it back to her. "Thanks a lot, Krithi. You understand me, what I want, and when I need it. Thanks a lot."

Karthik then turned to the couple and said, "Rajiv, ready? 1, 2, Click!"

After visiting the Taj Mahal, they went for lunch and then for shopping. Everyone was busy selecting items, while Karthik was focused on capturing Krithi's excitement as she looked at the things she liked.

Karthik bought a small Taj Mahal replica that fascinated him. He placed it in his bag, thinking that the white monument looked like a red symbol of love in his eyes. He then asked Radhika and Krithi to choose bangles for his mother and his two childhood friends.

"You have two girlfriends, Karthik?" Radhika teased.

"No, Bhabhi. They are my childhood friends," he replied with a smile. Both Radhika and Krithi laughed and picked a few sets of bangles.

By evening, they had to leave Saddar Market, return to the hotel to check out, and head to the train station. They all reached Delhi Railway Station. Karthik had an early morning flight to Hyderabad for work, so he had to leave soon. But before that, he went to the station to see everyone off.

Devyani and Rajiv were traveling to Shimla the same night. As everyone boarded the train, Karthik, Rajiv, and Devyani took blessings from the elders and said their goodbyes.

For Karthik, it was hard to leave Krithi and Seethu, but he thought to himself, *Long-distance relationships have their own beauty.* He knew he had to express his love for Krithi soon.

As the train departed with a loud whistle, Karthik watched it go, determined to share his feelings with her at the right moment.

Karthik, Rajiv, and Devyani went their separate ways according to their flight schedules. When Karthik reached Hyderabad, his brother picked him up. After freshening up, Karthik slept for a few hours since he had to go to the office early.

While having breakfast, he spoke with his mother.

"Maa, I have a lot to talk to you about. I'll come home early in the evening, and we can talk then. Finish your cooking and other work before I arrive."

"Is it that important, Karthik?" she asked.

"Yes, Maa. I need to discuss two important matters with you. And no, it's not about marriage," he added with a smile. "The couple's wedding was wonderful, and I had a great time. But more importantly, I discovered something interesting. I'll tell you in the evening."

Karthik then got up, washed his hands, and hurried to the office.

At the office, he met Prasad, discussed work, and then had a meeting with the manager about the project. The entire team was busy, as they had to submit the project draft for approval. In the rush, they worked hard and finally sent the project to the higher authorities by 6:30 PM.

After work, Karthik went home and asked his mother for tea and some snacks. She brought them for both of them.

"Maa, let's go upstairs and talk," he said, taking her hand. She followed him to the terrace, where they both sat down.

"What happened, beta? Why all this secrecy? We could have talked inside the house too," his mother asked.

"No, Maa. This is very confidential and important. No one should know until the right time," Karthik said seriously.

"Okay, okay. First, drink your tea. We'll talk after that," she said with a smile.

"Now tell me, Karthik, what happened?" his mother asked.

"Maa, Sarath bro's wife, Radhika bhabhi, has another sibling apart from her and Krithi. But he went missing in childhood when he was just four years old. They are searching from more than 30years but he didn't found. He had a unique ability—whenever he saw a photo, he could tell the name of the cameraman."

His mother was surprised. "Is that true?"

"Yes, Maa," Karthik nodded.

"How do you know this, Karthik?" she asked.

Karthik then told her the story about Krithi's father's lost wallet. He also shared his suspicion. "Maa, do you remember that Ramaa aunty's elder son Govind also had this same ability? Lakshman once told me that his brother was adopted, but he is very loving and caring. I think they might be the same person. But I didn't tell anyone yet because I want to be sure first. What do you think?"

His mother nodded thoughtfully. "That sounds correct, Karthik. It's amazing to hear, but also sad. Ramaa aunty loves her elder son a lot. If she finds out, it might break her heart. This is a very sensitive matter, and we need to be careful about how we reveal it. First, we must confirm whether the missing boy is really Govind or not. I'll visit Ramaa aunty's home a few times, observe her emotions, and gather more information to connect the dots."

"Okay, Maa, that's what I wanted to share. I feel relieved now because I've been holding onto this secret for so long."

His mother smiled. "Good. Now, what's the second thing you wanted to tell me?"

Karthik smiled and said, "Maa, the wedding was amazing. From the first day of preparations to their honeymoon, everything was perfect. Our trip was wonderful too. Watching the couple and seeing how their families welcomed them made me feel like marriage is a beautiful thing. Isn't it, Maa?"

His mother chuckled. "That's nice to hear, Karthik, but tell me what you really wanted to say."

Karthik took a deep breath. "Maa, you know Radhika bhabhi's sister, Krithi?"

"Yes."

"I love her. I like her a lot, Maa. If she agrees, I want to marry her—with your blessing."

His mother's face lit up. "Wow, that's wonderful news, Karthik! Show me her photo."

Karthik showed Krithi's picture. His mother admired it. "She looks so beautiful and innocent. Perfect for you, Karthik! When can I talk to her?"

Karthik shook his head. “Maa, I haven’t taken any photos with her. I decided not to until she accepts my proposal.”

His mother smiled. “That’s good, Karthik. Call her once, I’ll talk to her.”

“Maa, please wait. My story isn’t over yet. She is going to the U.S. to complete her MS.”

“What? That will take two years!” his mother exclaimed.

“Yes, Maa,” Karthik sighed.

“So what now? Do we have to wait for another two to three years?” she asked.

“Maa, please. I really like Krithi. I haven’t even told her about my feelings yet—I wanted to share it with you first.”

“Okay, thanks for telling me,” his mother said. “Propose to her as soon as possible. First, make sure she doesn’t have anyone in her life.”

“She doesn’t, Maa. She told me herself, and even Devyani confirmed it.”

His mother smiled. “Oh, you’ve gone too far, my son.”

Karthik smiled back. “She will be coming to Hyderabad for shopping, and she’ll visit our home too. I’ll let you know when.”

“Alright, Karthik. Is there anything else? Your dad will be home soon.”

“No, Maa. I feel much more relaxed now. Thank you for understanding me.”

His mother patted his shoulder. “I know my son, and I respect his decisions. Come, have lunch and take a nap. You didn’t sleep well last night. Tomorrow, I’ll visit Ramaa aunty’s home.”

“Okay, Maa, let’s go,” Karthik said.

They both went downstairs together.

From that day onwards, Karthik’s mother visited Rama Aunty’s house several times, and they went shopping together. One day, as they sat and had a conversation, Rama Aunty started praising Govind a lot. Karthik’s mother asked, "Rama, do you like Govind more than Lakshman? Is there a special reason?"

Rama replied, "Yes, he is very special to us. He is a gift from God. Lakshman came into my life through birth, but Govind came by God's wish to fulfill something special for me and my husband. We were praying to God, asking for a child. One day, my husband and I went to the Jagannatha temple. After the darshan, we found Govind crying. We asked him who his parents were and where he was from, but he couldn't answer because he was only 3 or 4 years old. So, we decided to announce his presence over the temple's loudspeaker, but no one came. After a long time, we went to the police station to ask if there were any missing child reports. The officer said he would inform us, but we never heard back. That's when we thought maybe God wanted us to keep this child with us.

We began raising him, and over time, we noticed that he had extraordinary focus. He could observe things deeply, even more than we could. We thought he could do well in investigation or CBI-related jobs, where such skills could benefit society. He grew up to be a kind and responsible person, taking care of Lakshman and his other siblings. Once he was old enough to understand, my husband and I told him the story of how we found him at the Jagannath temple.

What did he say? Karthik's mother asked.

Rama replied, "He understood what had happened, but he said he didn't want to meet his birth parents because we raised him as our own. However, if they ever came looking for him, he would accept them as his parents, too."

"Govind is very mature, isn't he?" Karthik's mother remarked.

"Yes, he is," Rama replied.

Then Karthik's mother asked, "What if Govind's real parents came and asked you to send him with them? What would you do?"

Rama took a deep breath and said, "Since they gave birth to Govind, if they came to take him, we would have to send him with them, but only if Govind agrees. What else can we do?" Her eyes filled with tears.

Karthik's mother quickly apologized, "I'm so sorry, I didn't mean to hurt you by asking that."

Rama smiled softly, "No, it's okay, dear. We've had this fear for a long time."

Just then, Karthik arrived to pick up his mother. Their conversation ended, and they both moved on.

When Karthik's mother got into the car, Karthik asked, "Maa, how is Rama Aunty? Did you find out anything from her?"

"Yes, dear, it's very hard to hear. If Govind is sent back to his real parents, Rama Aunty and Uncle still have that fear inside them. I felt very sad hearing that. And yes, Govind was found at the Jagannatha temple. They tried to send him to his parents, but couldn't find them, so they thought maybe God sent Govind to them."

"Oh, okay, Maa. Then we'll arrange a meeting for both families, so they can meet each other, and hopefully, their fears will go away," Karthik suggested.

"Stop it, Karthik. Why are you deciding so quickly? The only common thing we know about both families is that Govind was found at the temple and that he has great focus. That's it. What other evidence do you have to decide this?" Karthik's mother asked.

Karthik replied, "Maa, as I told you, I've seen Govind's childhood photo, and it's the same one I saw at Rama Aunty's house."

"Is it? Are you sure?" Karthik's mother asked, with excitement.

"Yes, Maa, it's the same photo. I saw it on Lakshman's laptop this morning when he came to me with a question. I'm sure, Maa," Karthik confirmed.

"That's good then. We'll arrange the meeting. But before that, let's go to Vizag and see how they feel. After that, we'll decide when to arrange the family get-together."

"Okay, Maa. We'll go this weekend," Karthik agreed.

"Wait, wait... you just came this week. Now you're going again this weekend? For Kirthi?" she teased.

"No, Maa, this time it's for Govind," he smiled.

Karthik and his mother went home and continued their usual routine. When the weekend came, they traveled to Vizag. Their first stop was at Sarath's home, where they met and chatted for a while, and had lunch together. After that, they went to Krithi's home.

Krithi was surprised to see Karthik there. She looked at him with excitement, which Karthik's mother noticed.

Karthik introduced his mother to Krithi's parents. Then Krithi went up to Karthik's mother and took her blessings. Karthik's mother lifted Krithi and hugged her, asking, "How are you, dear?"

"I'm fine, aunty. How are you?" Krithi replied.

"All good, dear," Karthik's mother said. Then she quietly asked Karthik, "She is very beautiful. But I'm sad, Why is she still calling me aunty?"

"Maa, I told you, I haven't proposed to her yet. Please stay calm. We came here for another reason, not for your daughter-in-law," Karthik jokingly replied.

Everyone sat together, and Krithi's mother brought snacks and tea for them. As they were talking, Krithi's mother invited Karthik and his mother to stay for two days.

"No, aunty, we came to Vizag for other work. I just wanted to introduce my mother to all of you, that's why we came here. so we need to leave tonight," Karthik explained.

Karthik's mother asked by pointing a photo frame on the wall, "Is Virat the one Karthik mentioned, your son?"

"Yes, he is my son," Krithi's mother replied.

The conversation moved to another topic, and Karthik's mother invited Krithi's family to come to Hyderabad. "Come to Hyderabad sometime. We'll have fun."

Krithi's mother replied, "Yes, we will come. Krithi is flying abroad, but she will come to Hyderabad alone for shopping. She has friends there to meet, and then she'll come to your house."

Krithi nodded and looked at Karthik. Their eyes met, and they shared a special moment. Karthik's mother gently touched his shoulder. "Karthik, shall we go? Remember, we came for another reason," she chuckled.

As they were leaving, Karthik's mother asked Krithi's mother, "Can I ask you something, if you don't mind?"

"Yes, of course," Krithi's mother replied.

Karthik's mother asked, "What if Virat's real parents came to meet him? Would you ask him to go with them?"

Krithi's mother answered, "That's his choice. We can't tell him to leave them. We don't know what his situation is. If he's okay, we'll ask him to visit us sometimes, but we understand the pain of a son being far away from us."

Karthik's mother nodded, "I'm sorry for asking, but thank you for your answer."

"It's okay, take care," Krithi's mother said.

Karthik and his mother got into the car and said goodbye to Krithi and her parents. As they drove back, Karthik and his mother had the answer and solution they needed to arrange a family meeting and bring them all together again. They returned to Hyderabad, and their usual routine began again.

Krithi texted Karthik,

Krithi: Hey, did you reach Hyderabad? And why did you come suddenly without informing me?

Him: Yes, we reached. Going to the office now. After a while, we need to sleep for some time.

Krithi: If you had told me that your mother was coming with you, I could have been more prepared.

Him: Why do you need to get ready? You're already beautiful.

Krithi: stop it Karthik. Just casually asking. Ok take rest bye.

A few days later, Krithi texted Karthik saying that she would be coming to Hyderabad in a week and staying for three days, but she wouldn't be staying at Karthik's house. She wanted to meet her friends, but she planned to go shopping with Karthik. Both Karthik and Krithi were excited to see each other, though Krithi wasn't confessing her feelings to him. Karthik, eager to spend time with her, started planning for the day they would meet, asking his childhood girl friends for advice on where to go shopping and what would be best for a girl.

Krithi, on the other hand, was feeling happy but also telling herself not to think too much about Karthik. She reminded herself to focus on her studies, but still, thoughts of Karthik kept coming to her mind, and her heart was filled with happiness. It felt like a balloon about to burst with excitement as she thought about meeting him and spending time together.

Karthik informed his mother that Krithi was coming next week. "Oh, that's nice! Karthik, get ready, take a leave, and keep your room clean. Otherwise, she'll be shocked to see how messy your everyday life is," she chuckled. "Maa..." Karthik smiled.

A week later, Krithi arrived in Hyderabad, and Karthik went to pick her up and drop her at her friend's house. She said, "I'll call you tomorrow. We'll go shopping and maybe visit a coffee shop. By the way, will your boss give you leave?" Then she added, "Oh, I forgot! Your boss is great; I know he will give it to you. If not, just tell him your friend is asking you to come."

"Yeah, I'll tell him I need to go out with my girlfriend and need a leave," Karthik said.

"Your girlfriend?" Krithi asked.

"Yes, you are a girl and my friend. What's wrong with that?" Karthik smiled.

Krithi nodded and said, "Bye, I'll meet you tomorrow. Today, I'll spend time with my friends. I'll call you to pick me up for shopping."

Krithi was chilling with her friends at home because they didn't want to waste even a minute traveling somewhere. They made arrangements to stay in, so they could relax and share their feelings with each other. Meanwhile, Krithi's friends asked her about Karthik. "He looks smart, just like you said. We thought he would look bored, but he's actually really good," they chuckled.

"Of course, he is," Krithi smiled.

Her friends teased her, saying, "hey hey hey... are you in love with him? Tell us seriously!"

Krithi quickly replied, "No, I don't have any thoughts like that, but Karthik is a good person. I just don't want to get into a relationship too soon and let it affect my education and career. I'm not saying that Karthik would spoil anything—I just don't want any distractions."

Her friends asked, "What if he doesn't wait for you until you finish your studies? His mother is already looking for a bride for him."

"Krithi, we're serious," one of her friends added. "We've known you since childhood, and you've never spoken positively about a boy or trusted one easily. But we saw you talking about Karthik at the wedding, and you even traveled with him, even though it wasn't your city. And now you're saying, 'If he doesn't wait'? Does that mean if he does wait, you'd be okay with it?"

Her friends surrounded her, pressing for an answer.

"Hey, why are you guys stressing about this? Change the topic," Krithi said, trying to avoid the conversation.

"No, Krithi, you have to decide," her friends insisted. "Don't take your life for granted. If you think he's right for you and your family, then tell him to wait for you."

"I don't even know what his feelings are," Krithi admitted.

"Then find out before you leave India!" one of her friends said.

"I don't know, dear," Krithi said honestly. "When I talk to him, my heart feels light, like the wind flowing gently. There's an unknown excitement in my eyes. Even after our conversations, his words keep echoing in my ears until someone else speaks to me. But if I let these feelings grow, my studies might get affected. That's why I don't want to admit anything to myself before I talk to him."

"Just think about it, Krithi. Take this seriously. We can't be sure if guys will stay the same in the future, and nowadays, we're surrounded by so many bad ones. If you find a good one, don't let him go," one of her friends suggested. "You're going shopping with him tomorrow and visiting his home, so just observe and think about your future."

"Okay, fine," Krithi replied to avoide the topic.

"Let's have lunch now. Come on," another friend said, patting her shoulder.

Later, they finished their lunch and had fun the entire day.

Before going to bed, Karthik texted Krithi.

Karthik: "Hey, what are you doing? Did you have dinner?"

Krithi: "Yes, I had. What about you?"

Karthik: "I had dinner too. Mom was asking when you will come home. What should I tell her?"

Krithi: "We'll go after shopping, around 4 O clock." Come Around 10 O clock.

Karthik: "Okay. I'll come tomorrow around 10 AM. We'll start then?"

Krithi: "Yes, that's fine."

Karthik: "Alright, I'll call you once I reach there."

Krithi: "Okay. Good night, Karthik."

Karthik: "Good night, dear."

He put his phone away and went to sleep.

But both Karthik and Krithi couldn't sleep for a while. They watched reels, listened to songs, and kept trying to sleep. Eventually, they dozed off.

Karthik woke up around 6 AM and texted Krithi

Karthik: Good morning, Krithi

Krithi: GM, Karthik. (Seen at 7:30 AM)

Karthik: Hey Krithi, can we meet earlier than 10 o'clock?

Krithi: Why? My friends told me malls and stores only open around 10 AM.

Karthik: Yes, of course. But before that, can we go for a small ride? We can go to a mall that's farther away so we can spend more time talking.

Krithi: Oh, I see. Okay. What time will you come then?

Karthik: Can I come at 8 o'clock?

Krithi: Hey Karthik, it's 7:34 now! How can I get ready so fast? I haven't even had breakfast yet!

Karthik: Hey, do one thing—let's have breakfast together at my favorite place, and then we'll go to the mall. Please, Krithi!

Krithi: Ahhhh... okay fine. I'll get ready.

Karthik: Yay! I'll be there soon.

Krithi: Okay, see you!

As soon as she said **"okay,"** Krithi put away her phone and rushed to get ready.

"Where's my bag? My towel? And what dress should I wear?" she asked her friends in a hurry.

"Hey, stop! Why are you rushing? You said you'd leave around 10 o'clock. What's the hurry?" her friends asked.

"Karthik just texted me. He's coming in an hour, and we're having breakfast together," Krithi said.

"Ohhh, your special someone is coming, huh?" her friends teased, chuckling.

"Stop it, guys! I'm going to take a bath," Krithi said and rushed inside to get ready.

While getting dressed, she noticed something—she was carefully choosing her outfit, matching accessories, and making sure everything looked good together. She had never paid attention to these things before.

She felt a wave of excitement and told herself, **"Hey Krithi, just be calm. Be calm."**

Karthik arrived and called Krithi to come out. Krithi and her friends stepped outside. As Krithi walked towards the car, Karthik got down, greeted her friends, and opened the car door for her. Then, he got into the car, adjusted the mirror, and waved goodbye to Krithi's friends.

"So, where do we go now?" Karthik asked.

"First, we'll buy sweatshirts and winter wear. After that, you decide where we should go," Krithi replied.

"What about casuals and formals?"

"I already bought those in Vizag. I came here to get these things and some stone jewelry from Charminar—and to spend time with my friends," she explained.

"Oh, okay. Then we'll go to Charminar in the evening. It looks better at night. Before that, after we finish shopping, we'll go to my home for lunch, meet my mom, and then head to Charminar. After that, I'll drop you off."

"Fine then," Krithi agreed.

They first went to **TFN**, Karthik's favorite restaurant.

"What do you want?" Karthik asked.

"Since it's your favorite place, you order. I'll be fine with anything," Krithi said.

"Okay then, I'll order something different!" Karthik said with a smile.

He ordered a **Red Velvet Dosa**. Krithi was surprised to see it.

"Karthik, I didn't even know Red Velvet Dosa existed!" she said in amazement.

Karthik smiled. **"Try it,"** he said.

Krithi took a bite and exclaimed, **"Wow, it's so good, Karthik! I love it! Usually, I'm not a foodie, but I really liked this. I want more!"**

Karthik laughed and ordered another one. After finishing their breakfast, he called his mother.

"Mom, Krithi and I will come for lunch," he said.

"You're both most welcome! What does she like? I'll prepare something for her," his mother asked.

Without hesitation, Karthik replied, **"She mostly likes veggies, Mom—like dal, aloo, and dishes like that."**

His mother chuckled. **"Oh, you already know? You're answering without even asking her!"**

Karthik smiled. **"Yes, Mom, I know."**

Then, he got into the car, and they continued their day.

After breakfast, they went to a coffee shop where Karthik had his first and most beautiful coffee with his loved one. He was really excited to spend the day with Krithi, and Krithi felt the same. They enjoyed a lovely conversation, not expressing their love with words but through their feelings, breaths, and looks. Unfortunately, they lost track of time while talking and didn't notice how much time had passed. It wasn't until Krithi's friend called her at around 11:30 AM.

Her friend asked, "Hey Krithi, will you and Karthik come for lunch? We'll be preparing it here."

Krithi replied, "Lunch? Isn't it too early for that?"

Her friend responded, "Early? It's already 11:30! Did you forget the time with Karthik? Haven't you done any shopping yet? I have my doubts," she chuckled.

Krithi quickly adjusted her voice and said, "Oh, nothing. I just went shopping for some clothes."

"Okay, okay, carry on," her friend said before ending the call.

After their heartwarming conversation, Karthik and Krithi stepped out of the coffee shop, still feeling the warmth of the moment. The cold air outside brought them back to reality, and they decided to continue their day by going shopping. Krithi was excited to pick out some new clothes, and she led the way into the store.

As they walked through the aisles, Krithi picked out a few sweatshirts and headed to the fitting room to try them on. She stood in front of the mirror, adjusting the clothes, and called out to Karthik, "What do you think? Does this look good on me?"

Karthik, ever the supportive companion, smiled and replied, "Everything looks good on you, Krithi. Seriously, everything suits you when you wear it."

Krithi laughed and tried on another sweatshirt, looking at herself in the mirror. "Are you sure? I can't decide between these two."

With a gentle smile, Karthik nodded. "I'm sure. You look amazing in both, but I think that blue one really brings out your smile."

Their shopping went on like this, with Krithi enjoying his compliments and Karthik happy to see her so excited. The playful back-and-forth continued as she picked out more clothes, asking for his opinion, and he replied with warm, genuine praise.

As they continued shopping, Krithi browsed through the saree section, looking for something special. She picked out two casual sarees for herself, carefully choosing colors and patterns she liked. But her shopping didn't stop there. She decided to pick a saree for her sister, one for Karthik's mother, and one for her own mother as well.

While she was picking out the sarees, Krithi turned to Karthik and asked, "Hey, what's your mom's favorite color? I want to buy a saree for her."

Karthik was a bit surprised but smiled at the thoughtful gesture. "You want to buy a saree for my mom?" he asked, his voice a mix of curiosity and appreciation.

Krithi smiled and nodded. "Yes, I really want to. I don't know why, but I just feel like getting her something nice. So, what's her favorite color?"

Karthik thought for a moment before answering. "She loves red. She mostly wears red sarees."

Krithi's eyes brightened as she picked up a red saree from the rack. "Perfect! I'll get her a beautiful red one then."

With that, Krithi continued to carefully select the sarees, making sure each one was perfect. She felt a special joy in choosing something thoughtful for the people she cared about, and Karthik couldn't help but appreciate how much effort she was putting into it.

Once the sarees were all picked out, Krithi smiled contently, feeling happy with her choices. She knew that these gifts would mean a lot to both her and Karthik's family. And as she enjoyed her shopping, Karthik enjoyed simply watching her—lost in her enthusiasm, her excitement making the moment even more special.

Once they finished shopping, their bags in hand, they decided to head to Karthik's house for lunch. The afternoon was still young, but both of them were content with the day so far, ready to enjoy a quiet meal together.

As they walked towards the billing counter, Krithi turned to Karthik with a playful grin. "You know, I think I might have gone a little overboard," she admitted, glancing at the stack of sarees in her hands.

Karthik chuckled. "A little? You just turned a simple shopping trip into a full-fledged saree festival," he teased.

Krithi laughed, nudging him lightly. "Hey, don't make fun of me! I just love picking gifts."

"I can see that," Karthik said, smiling. Then, after a brief pause, he added softly, "It's really sweet of you."

Krithi looked up at him, a little surprised by the sincerity in his voice. Their eyes met for a moment, a quiet warmth settling between them.

Breaking the silence, Karthik cleared his throat and grabbed a small box from a nearby counter. “Since you love gifting, let me return the favor,” he said, handing it to her.

Krithi blinked, taken aback. “What is this?” she asked curiously.

“Open it and see,” Karthik said with a smirk.

It was a sleek, tailored coat with a formal look. Krithi loved it instantly and smiled as she thanked Karthik. She decided to keep it and bring it with her to the USA. Surprisingly, she felt even happier about this coat than the sarees she had carefully picked out.

She couldn’t wait to wear it, to wrap herself in its warmth—but now wasn’t the time. They were already at the billing counter, and they were running late for lunch. With a content sigh, she held onto the coat, knowing she would cherish it when the right moment came.

Both got into the car, and Karthik started driving. Krithi asked, "What else do we need to buy? Is everything done?"

Karthik replied, "What? No, we haven’t even finished half of the shopping yet! You kept taking me to coffee shops and for breakfast. That’s all we got done!"

Karthik smiled and said, "But every minute is beautiful to me. I enjoyed this day."

Krithi laughed and said, "You might be the first man to say that, Karthik. Men usually don’t encourage girls to shop. That’s why girls go shopping with their friends. But you came with me. Thank you so much, Karthik. Thank you for everything—from rescuing Seethu to now. You mean a lot to us. We never think of you as someone from another family. You’re part of ours. Thank you so much!"

Karthik smiled and said, "Hey, Krithi, you’re saying too much about me. Enough."

"Okay," Krithi said with a smile. "By the way, we’re still going to Charminar this evening, right?"

"Yes," Karthik replied.

They soon arrived at Karthik's house. They got out of the car, and Karthik's mom came out to greet Krithi. Krithi took her blessings, then went back to the car to get the bags, but Karthik's mom said, "Karthik will bring them, you come inside."

They both went inside and sat in the living room. Krithi loved the atmosphere of Karthik's house. It was filled with greenery, and the natural air made it feel refreshing. Even though they were in the city, the house had a traditional feel to it, and Krithi liked it a lot.

"Aunty, your house is so beautiful," Krithi said. "It feels so nice as soon as I walked in."

Karthik entered with the bags and handed them over to Krithi. "Here you go, everything safe," he said, smiling. Krithi thanked him and turned to Karthik's mom. "Aunty, you have a very beautiful home. It feels so peaceful here," Krithi said, admiring the surroundings.

Karthik's mom smiled warmly. "Thank you, dear. We're happy you like it. Please make yourself comfortable," she said, guiding Krithi to a chair.

Karthik then sat next to Krithi, feeling proud of his mom's hospitality. The atmosphere in the house felt calm and welcoming, with sunlight streaming in through the windows and plants adding a touch of nature.

Krithi relaxed, feeling at home, and chatted a bit more with Karthik's mom. "So, what do we have planned for this evening?" Krithi asked, eager to continue the day.

"We'll head to Charminar later, as we planned," Karthik replied. "But before that, you can rest for a while." Karthik mom said.

Krithi nodded, grateful for the peaceful moment. She couldn't help but feel a deep sense of belonging, knowing that Karthik and his family had welcomed her so warmly.

Karthik, Krithi, and Karthik's mom had lunch together and chatted for a while. After some time, Karthik's mom noticed that Krithi looked a bit tired.

“Krithi, why don't you go and rest for a bit?” she suggested. “You can relax, and later, you both can visit Charminar.”

"It's okay, Aunty, I'm fine," Krithi said, then added with a smile, "Why don't you come with us this evening?"

Karthik's mom smiled warmly. "You both enjoy your trip. We'll go out when your family visits. We can make a day of it—shopping, food, and everything! But for today, you and Karthik should finish your shopping."

She then stood up and said, "Come, let me show you to the bedroom." As they walked past Karthik's room, she pointed it out. Krithi took a quick glance inside—it was simple and neatly maintained, just as she had expected.

They reached the master bedroom, and Karthik's mom switched on the AC before turning to leave.

But Krithi called out, "Aunty, I'm not feeling sleepy. Can we just lie down and talk for a while? Would you stay with me?"

Karthik's mom smiled. "Why not, dear? I'd love to."

As they lay down and chatted, Krithi's eyes wandered to the framed photos in the room. She pointed to a picture of two young men and asked, "Is that Karthik's brother?"

Karthik's mom nodded. "Yes, that's his younger brother. He's in his final year of engineering. He's a Kannayya of this family. Kannayya name itself covers everything right? Karthik mother said with smile. Karthik, on the other hand, was always responsible and focused on his studies."

Krithi listened with interest, enjoying this new perspective on Karthik. She loved hearing about his childhood and family.

After a while, Karthik's mom said, "I'm so happy that Karthik has a good family, and I'm thankful to Seethu for bringing you into our lives."

Krithi smiled and replied, "Aunty, I'm lucky to have you in my life too. These days, many women misunderstand the new girls coming into their family, but you're so kind and understanding. You've raised your children so well—especially Karthik.

`She continued, "My mom and dad like Karthik a lot. After our trip to Delhi, my mom couldn't stop talking about him! Even my sisters' families adore him."

Karthik's mom beamed with happiness, touched by Krithi's words. Krithi felt proud to share how much her family cherished Karthik. This conversation made her feel even more connected to his family, strengthening their bond.

After a while, Karthik and Krithi were about to leave when Karthik's mom suddenly called out to Krithi and stopped her. She went inside and returned with a beautiful saree.

"This is for you," she said warmly, handing it to Krithi. Then, as a traditional gesture, she applied sindoor to Krithi's forehead, since it was her first visit to their home.

Krithi accepted the saree with gratitude, feeling blessed. Karthik stood beside them, watching with pride, admiring his mother's deep-rooted traditions.

Karthik then picked up Krithi's bags, getting ready to leave. Krithi smiled and said goodbye to Karthik's mom, thanking her before they finally set off for Charminar.

When they arrived at Charminar, it was crowded. The streets were full of people, and many shops had brightly lit displays with dresses and bangles. The air was filled with the sweet scents of attar and street food. They parked the car a little further away and walked towards the busy market. Krithi couldn't help but stare at the dresses and bangles sparkling in the evening light while snacking on treats from the street vendors. Meanwhile, Karthik kept an eye on her, carefully protecting her from the bustling crowd.

Krithi spotted a shop and pointed it out to Karthik. They went inside, and Krithi started selecting bangles. She smiled and said, "Karthik, I like all the bangles in this shop! I don't know which one to choose."

Karthik smiled back and said, "Buy whatever you want, Krithi. It's your choice. And if you're having trouble paying, just let me know. I'll take care of it."

After choosing a few bangles for the women in their family, they moved on to another shop that was famous for its bangles, called *Matti Gajulu*. Krithi picked out a set of blue bangles and asked the shopkeeper for them.

As Krithi tried to wear the bangles, she struggled a little. The shopkeeper asked Karthik to help her. Karthik gently helped her put the bangles on. As he did, he felt his heart beating faster and his emotions rising. It was a very special moment for him, as the girl he wanted to marry was asking him for help with something so simple. It was an emotional experience for every man, and Karthik was happy to help.

Krithi noticed his hands were trembling slightly and his heartbeat was faster than usual. She smiled to herself, knowing how much this moment meant to him.

Later, they went to visit the historical site, Charminar. They climbed a few steps and took some photos since it is a famous landmark. After that, they came down, had some snacks, and then went to drink Irani chai.

After their outing, they returned to Krithi's friend's home to drop her off. Meanwhile, Karthik said, "It was a wonderful journey, Krithi. Thank you so much for this day."

Krithi smiled and replied, "Even for me, Karthik. Thank you so much for being beside me."

Karthik smiled and asked, "When will we meet again?"

Krithi said, "Only when I fly to the USA. I'll come with my family."

Hearing that she would only meet him when she was leaving, Karthik's mood suddenly changed. He felt sad knowing that she would be so far away for the next two years. He became quiet and continued driving.

Noticing his silence, Krithi asked, "Why are you so quiet? You look dull. What happened?"

Karthik adjusted his voice and said, "Nothing, Krithi. I'm okay."

Soon, they reached Krithi's friend's home. Karthik dropped her off, but Krithi's friend invited him inside for coffee. He politely declined, but she insisted that he should stay for dinner. Krithi also asked him to join, so Karthik agreed and went inside.

Once he sat down, Karthik called his mother to inform her that he would have dinner at Krithi's friend's home. Hearing this, Krithi was impressed that he took the time to inform his mother since she would be waiting for him for dinner.

After dinner, Karthik left after saying goodbye. Krithi's friend assured her that they would drop her off at the railway station.

Karthik left with a heavy heart, knowing she wouldn't be around for two years. Krithi felt the same weight in her heart but didn't express it to anyone.

The next day, Krithi returned home. As the days passed quickly, she focused on preparing to go abroad for her studies. She made arrangements, met her friends, family friends, and relatives, and spent special time with her sister and Seethu.

Meanwhile, Karthik's mother was keeping track of Govind's mother, Ramaa, and Krithi's mother, observing their emotions. She wanted to reveal that Govind was actually Virat, the child Krithi's parents had lost in his childhood.

As Krithi's departure grew closer, she started packing her luggage and preparing herself to stay alone in a foreign country without her family. Her parents, sister Radhika, and brother-in-law Sarath, and Devyani decided to accompany her to Hyderabad. They also planned to visit Karthik's home before she left.

Finally, the day arrived when Krithi had to leave her home and begin her journey to Hyderabad. Both families—Krithi's and her relatives—were ready to travel. Sarath, her brother-in-law, informed Karthik that they were on their way. Karthik, feeling excited, responded warmly, "Wow, that's great! You're most welcome, brother. We'll be waiting for you."

After that, Karthik's mother took the phone and spoke to Sarath, expressing her happiness. "I will be the happiest person when both our families meet. We are eagerly waiting for you. Please come soon, beta."

The very next day, both Krithi's family and Sarath's family reached Hyderabad. Karthik and his father went to receive them, and everyone made their way to Karthik's home. It was a moment Krithi had been eagerly anticipating, as she finally saw Karthik again after such a long time. However, even though they were finally together, Karthik seemed a little distant, almost as if something was weighing on his mind.

Everyone at the house noticed his change in behavior and asked him, "Why are you so dull today? You're usually so active and cheerful with us. What happened?"

But Karthik didn't respond. He remained silent, trying to hide his emotions. Krithi, however, noticed the change in his mood. She could see the heaviness in his eyes and wondered what might be troubling him.

Karthik's cousin, Sharanya, also arrived at the house, and as she settled in, Karthik's mother asked her to keep Krithi and Devyani company. "Sharanya, why don't you spend some time with Krithi and Devyani? Help them feel more at home," she said kindly.

Sharanya, Devyani, and Krithi shared the same room for the next two days. After they had freshened up and introduced their families to each other while having lunch, Karthik's mother invited Ramaa's family for a nice dinner on same day. While the preparations were underway, Krithi found herself rechecking her luggage, feeling anxious and emotional. The thought of leaving her family behind and flying abroad to study was making her uneasy.

Sharanya and Devyani noticed the worry on Krithi's face. They could sense she was overwhelmed, and they decided to keep her company. Sharanya started a conversation with her, trying to ease her anxiety while Devyani also in a mood of missing krithi.

Meanwhile, there was a knock on the door. It was Karthik. "Can I come in?" he asked. Sharanya glanced at Krithi to check if she was okay with Karthik joining them. Seeing Krithi nod, she replied, "You can come in, brother."

Karthik entered the room holding two packages in his hands. One was filled with chocolates and snacks, carefully packed for Krithi to take with her on her journey abroad. The other was a special gift.

He handed her the chocolates and snacks first, smiling gently. "I thought you might like these for your travels," he said. Krithi took them with a heavy heart, unsure of how to feel. She said, "Thanks," but deep inside, she felt conflicted. She couldn't help but wonder if she was doing the right thing. Karthik's feelings for her seemed to be growing stronger, but she was leaving the country without ever confessing her own feelings for him.

Karthik looked at her, his expression serious. "Krithi, I need to talk to you," he began, his voice steady but filled with emotion. "I know we're in my home, but I can't hold back anymore. There's something I need to say."

He turned to her sister, Devyani, and said, "Could you close the door, please?"

Devyani and Sharanya, understanding the seriousness of the moment, stood up to leave the room. But Karthik stopped them, saying, "No, you guys can stay inside, but please close the door. It's important."

Devyani and Sharanya nodded and closed the door, standing to the side, giving Karthik and Krithi the privacy they needed.

Karthik then handed Krithi the second package: a small, elegant gift. It was a white polished Taj Mahal, with a clock placed on the upper part of it, surrounded by beautiful blue roses. The gift was simple, yet it carried so much meaning. Karthik knelt down in front of her, his eyes filled with sincerity.

"Krithi," he began, his voice trembling slightly. "I love you. I want to marry you. Please don't worry—it's not going to happen right now. Once you finish your studies, we'll get married, if that's okay with you."

Krithi felt her heart skip a beat. She hadn't expected this at all. Her mind raced as she tried to process his words.

Karthik continued, his voice soft but filled with deep emotion. "I couldn't keep these feelings inside any longer," he said, his words carrying the weight of everything he had kept bottled up for so long. "My heart feels so heavy, but now, after telling you, I feel a bit of relief. I've been waiting for this moment, and I've been holding onto this gift ever since we visited the Taj Mahal together. I found it there and thought it would be the perfect way to express my feelings. I kept it all this time, waiting for the right moment to give it to you."

Krithi, stunned and surprised by the depth of his words, stood frozen. She was taken aback, not expecting such an intimate confession. Karthik gently placed the small gift in her hands, his eyes never leaving hers. "Please accept this gift, Krithi," he said. "It's a reminder that every morning, I'll be thinking of you, hoping that someday we can be together. This clock, shaped like the Taj Mahal, is my way of saying that I'll always remember you, no matter where life takes us."

Krithi's mind raced as she processed the sincerity in his voice. She could feel the weight of his emotions, yet her heart was conflicted. Karthik looked up at her, his gaze searching hers for any sign of understanding, any sign that she might feel the same. "I don't want to pressure you, Krithi," he added. "I truly love you, and I don't want to lose you. Please don't mind me taking the chance to propose. I just wanted to share my feelings with you, before it's too late."

Krithi felt her chest tighten. She was completely stunned, unsure of what to say or do. She had never imagined that Karthik would confess his love like this, especially at a time when she was preparing to leave the country for her studies. The words he had spoken overwhelmed her, and her mind struggled to process them.

She stood there in shock, unable to respond immediately. Her heart ached as she thought about the difficult decision she had to make. Was she ready to think about love right now? With so much going on in her life, she couldn't let herself get distracted.

After a long, heavy silence, Krithi took a few moments to collect her thoughts. Finally, she spoke. "Karthik, please stand up," she said softly. Karthik, who had been kneeling in front of her, slowly rose to his feet, his eyes still filled with hope and vulnerability.

Krithi took a deep breath, gathering her courage. "As I told you before, Karthik," she began, her voice steady but filled with regret, "I need to concentrate on my studies. I've made this commitment, and I don't want to get distracted by love right now. I'm sorry, but I have to focus on my future." She paused, feeling the weight of her words.

"I don't think badly of you, Karthik," she continued. "You've shared your feelings, and I truly appreciate that. But I can't say that I'll wait for you or that I can confirm your love for me. I'm not sure about love right now. I've never thought about it this way before. Please don't wait for me. I can't ask you to do that."

There was a long pause as Krithi processed the heaviness of the moment. She then added, "But I'll accept your gift, as it's from a good friend, and I will always cherish it as a memory of our friendship." With a gentle smile, she accepted the gift, holding it close to her chest.

Karthik, unable to find any words that could ease the pain in his heart, simply nodded. "I'll wait for you, Krithi... forever," he said softly, his voice almost breaking. He turned and left the room, his heart heavy with the weight of her rejection.

As Karthik walked out of the room, his face etched with emotion, he didn't notice that Radhika, Krithi's sister, had been watching him. She had seen the pain in his eyes and the sadness in his posture. She could tell that he was deeply affected by the conversation, and it made her heart ache for him.

Radhika stood silently in the hallway, watching him disappear down the corridor. She knew that Karthik's feelings for Krithi were genuine, and seeing him leave the room so emotionally drained made her realize just how much he truly cared for her sister. But at that moment, it was clear that Krithi was not ready to reciprocate those feelings. The weight of the situation hung in the air, and Radhika couldn't help but wonder what would happen next.

Radhika entered the room, her eyes scanning Krithi with concern. "Why is Karthik looking so dull?" she asked, her voice laced with worry. "Is everything okay? Did you hurt him?" She glanced down at the gift in Krithi's hands, noticing how it was almost being clutched, as if it carried a heavy weight.

Krithi sighed, her fingers brushing lightly over the gift as she replied softly, "Karthik proposed to me, sis."

Radhika's eyes widened in surprise. "Oh! What did you say? Do you have feelings for him?" Her voice was a mixture of curiosity and concern, as she watched Krithi's expression closely, trying to gauge her emotions.

Krithi sat down, her shoulders drooping slightly as she began explaining, "Sister, for me, studies come first. The real reason I came here was to go abroad. I've always wanted that for myself. And when I visited last time, Karthik's mom kindly invited me to their home, which is why I came. But... leave all that aside. Just answer me—do you have feelings for him?" She looked at Radhika with a faint, uncertain smile, her voice trailing off.

Radhika leaned against the doorframe, her expression thoughtful. She knew Krithi well enough to see the inner conflict in her. "Stop thinking too much. You're only confusing yourself," she said gently, her tone reassuring. "Just think about your future. If you want to be with him, I'll talk to Dad and see if we can arrange the marriage. Karthik is a good guy, and his family is really nice. We could ask them to wait until you finish your studies. It would give you time to focus and figure things out. I hadn't really thought about Karthik's proposal before, but there's nothing wrong with the idea. He seems like a good match for you."

Krithi sat quietly, her heart racing a little. She hadn't expected Radhika's response to be so understanding, so open. She smiled softly, feeling a weight lift off her shoulders. The relief that washed over her was almost tangible, as if she had been carrying an unseen burden that Radhika had just lightened. She hadn't made up her mind about Karthik, but the reassurance from her sister made the whole situation feel less overwhelming.

"Thank you, akka," Krithi whispered, her voice barely audible but filled with gratitude.

Radhika smiled back, stepping closer and giving her a quick, comforting hug. "Of course, I'm always here for you. Take your time. There's no rush to decide anything. We'll figure it out together."

Krithi's smile widened, and for the first time in a while, she felt like she could breathe a little easier. The uncertainty was still there, but with Radhika by her side, it didn't seem as daunting.

"Come, Kirthi and Devyani, let's go out and help Aunty. A few more guests are coming today, and she's making arrangements for us. Let's give her a hand. It will also help you relax and take your mind off things," Radhika said.

Hearing this, Kirthi carefully placed the gift in her luggage bag and quickly ran after Radhika. Seeing her do so, Radhika smiled, realizing that Kirthi liked the proposal but was thinking about her studies.

Both Kirthi and Devyani followed Radhika into the kitchen.

Meanwhile, Karthik's mom said, **"Please take rest, I will handle the arrangements with the help of our neighbor."** But Radhika and her sisters still went to help her. Together, they finished cooking and preparing everything for tonight's dinner.

Afterward, she turned to Kirthi and said, "Kirthi, you should go and rest. You have a long flight ahead, and you'll be exhausted. Don't worry, we will manage everything with Radhika."

Then she told Devyani, "Devyani, please go with Kirthi. If there's anything left to arrange for tomorrow, like packing luggage, help her with it and let her rest for a while."

Radhika was surprised to hear this, as she herself wished for Karthik and Kirthi to get married.

Devyani and Krithi walked into the room, and Krithi immediately sat down on the bed, feeling overwhelmed by a swirl of emotions. Her heart was heavy. She was missing her family, feeling the absence of Karthik, and struggling with her feelings for him. She couldn't bring herself to fully accept his love, and this confusion had caused her to hurt him with her words earlier. She regretted her harsh reply and was now lost in her thoughts.

Noticing Krithi's mood, Devyani walked over to her with a concerned look. She sat beside Krithi and gently called her name, "Krithi... why are you looking so dull? You've already shared your feelings, and Karthik has expressed his. There's no point in overthinking it. Don't keep everything on your mind right now. Just enjoy these two days and let things unfold. After that, you can think more clearly about everything. Trust me, my brother will never go after another girl. He's true to you, I know him well," Devyani reassured her.

Krithi, who had been holding back her tears, felt a sudden rush of comfort from Devyani's words. She hugged her tightly, her emotions now a mix of relief, sadness, and gratitude. Devyani's comforting words were exactly what Krithi needed to hear in that moment.

Meanwhile, in the living room, Karthik's father had just informed his wife that Ramaa's family had arrived. The family quickly got up and went to the living room to welcome them. It was time for introductions, and everyone greeted Ramaa's family warmly. Ramaa, her husband, and their two children—Govind and Lakshman—had arrived. After everyone had exchanged pleasantries, Lakshman, who seemed eager to catch up with Karthik, asked about him.

"Where's Karthik? I need to talk to him," Lakshman asked, scanning the room.

Lakshman made his way to Karthik's bedroom, knocking lightly on the door before stepping inside. "Hey, dude, what's going on? You look kind of dull. What's bothering you?" Lakshman asked, noticing Karthik's distracted expression.

Karthik gave a small, absent smile. "Nothing, man. Just... thinking," he replied, his voice trailing off as his mind wandered to Krithi and their earlier conversation.

"Did Ramaa aunty and Govind come?" Karthik asked, trying to change the subject.

"Yeah, they're here. Let's go to the living room," Lakshman replied. With that, the two of them left the bedroom and made their way downstairs to join the rest of the family in the living room.

Everyone gathered in the living room as Radhika and Karthik's mom served welcome drinks and snacks. Everyone took their seats, and after some time, they finished their dinner and sat back in the living room. Karthik played a video of Devyani's wedding and their honeymoon trip. He showed glimpses of the event, and everyone enjoyed watching it, reminiscing about the moments. Those who hadn't attended the wedding observed the images, while Govind asked, "Hey Karthik, did you also visit Ayodhya and the Taj Mahal? I don't see you in the pictures."

Karthik and his mom exchanged a glance, realizing their plan was about to be revealed. "There's no Karthik in the photos, how can you say that?" Karthik's father asked.

"I know, Uncle," Govind replied. Lakshman then joined the conversation and added, "Uncle, Govind has this unique ability. He can tell who is taking the picture just by observing closely."

Upon hearing this, Krithi's parents, Krithi, and Radhika exchanged looks. It was then that they realized Virat's identity. Krithi's parents were in tears as they asked about Govind, and inquired about his adoptive parents. Ramaa explained, "We found him at Jagannatha temple and tried to find his real parents, but we couldn't."

Karthik's mom took over the conversation, confirming that Govind is actually Virat, Krithi's brother, who was lost in childhood. "Ramaa, my best friend, adopted him and raised him to be such a good person," she said. "Karthik and I confirmed that Virat and Govind are the same person, and we arranged this gathering before Krithi going to the USA. Karthik wanted to give Krithi this precious moment."

Karthik's parents stood up and hugged both Govind and Karthik. The room became emotional, with Krithi also feeling overwhelmed. She felt proud of Karthik but couldn't look him in the eyes, especially since she had rejected his proposal earlier. However, she tried to express her gratitude with her eyes. Everyone praised Karthik and his mom.

Karthik's mom then added, "Ramaa, Govind's real parents didn't want to take him away from you. They knew that you had raised him as your own, and all they wanted was to be in touch with them and to take some responsibility for them. They didn't want to disturb the family you had formed, and they were happy with how well you had raised him."

Ramaa looked at Karthik's mom, relief washing over her face. She stepped forward, deeply moved by the trust and love in Karthik mom's words. She hugged her tightly, tears of gratitude in her eyes, and said, "Thank you. Thank you so much for sharing this with us. I feel so blessed."

The room was filled with emotion, and everyone stood in solidarity. Krithi watched in awe as she saw her brother, someone she had lost so many years ago, now standing before her, surrounded by people who loved him. She felt a rush of pride for Karthik, knowing how much effort he had put into bringing the truth to light. But there was also a lingering feeling of regret. She had rejected Karthik's proposal, and now, in this moment, she realized just how much he had done for her and her family.

She couldn't meet Karthik's eyes immediately, overwhelmed with emotion. But as she looked at him, she silently conveyed her gratitude with a soft sigh, her eyes speaking volumes.

Govind, Radhika, Krithi, and their parents were filled with excitement as they met him and shared many emotional moments. There was laughter, conversations, and heartfelt exchanges, making the time together even more special. However, after a while, it was time for Ramaa's family to leave. Everyone stepped outside to bid them farewell.

Before they left, Karthik's mother turned to Govind and said, "Why don't you stay back tonight with your parents?"

But Krithi's mother gently interrupted, "Not today. He can visit Vizag and stay with us anytime he wants."

With that, Govind joined Ramaa's family, and they left. The rest of them returned to Karthik's house, where everyone went to sleep—except for Krithi and Karthik.

Sleep didn't come easily to them. Krithi was leaving the next evening, and the weight of the farewell was pressing on both of them. Karthik's emotions were impossible to put into words. No one could understand his pain, and no one could feel the depth of his sorrow. It wasn't just about rejection—he had already accepted that—but the thought of missing Krithi was unbearable. He knew he could wait for her, no matter how long it took. After all, she was the only one he had ever loved—his first love.

Lost in their thoughts, they remained silent. Then, in the middle of the night, Devyani woke up, saw Krithi still awake, and gently pulled her close. “Sleep, Krithi,” she whispered, holding her comfortingly.

With that warmth, Krithi slowly drifted off to sleep. Karthik, too, eventually fell asleep, still lost in his thoughts.

The morning started with a quiet breakfast. The atmosphere was a mix of normalcy and unspoken emotions. After breakfast, the ladies decided to go shopping while the men left to check out some real estate sites.

As the group explored the stores, everyone seemed excited—except Krithi. She wandered through the shops without much interest. Radhika noticed and called her over.

“Krithi, come this way. Pick some dresses,” Radhika said, waving her towards a section.

Krithi shook her head lightly. “I don’t need any. I already bought some when I went shopping with Karthik last time.”

Radhika gave her a knowing smile. “Oh, are those enough?” she teased.

“Yes,” Krithi said, her voice soft. “They’re enough for me. I want to carry those memories with me.”

Radhika sighed and looked at her carefully. “Krithi, it seems like you love him and are really missing him. Just say the word, and we’ll arrange the marriage. Govind anna and I will talk to Mom and Dad. We’ll handle everything here.”

Krithi took a deep breath, her emotions stirring. “Please, akka... let it go. I just want to leave.”

Radhika held her hands. “If you and Karthik stay like this—so distant, so sad—it affects all of us. We feel it too. Please, think about it. But whatever happens, at least be happy today.”

Krithi didn’t say anything. Instead, she hugged her sister tightly.

After finishing their shopping, the ladies informed the men to meet them at a restaurant for lunch. Soon, both groups gathered at the restaurant, sharing a meal together.

Krithi chose to sit beside Karthik on purpose. She wanted to feel his presence, to take his warmth with her as a memory. Karthik, on the other hand, struggled to eat. His heart felt heavy, knowing that soon, she would be gone. The thought of missing her presence, her voice, her laughter—it all made the food tasteless.

After lunch, they all returned to Karthik's home. Krithi spent the remaining time with her family, Ramaa's family, and Karthik, cherishing every moment before her departure.

Finally, the moment arrived—it was time to leave for the airport.

All the elders like Krithi's parents were stay back at karthik home whereas Karthik, Devyani, Radhika and Govind went with her to drop her at Airport.

Krithi went to Govind and said, "Take care of mom and dad, bro. Bye, take care." Then she moved to Radhika and said, "Bye, akka. Take care of the family, especially Seethu, my charm." Finally, she went to Devyani, hugged her, and said, "Take care of your brother. He should be strong. From the first time I saw him, I felt he should be energetic, active, and the real star of the family. His aura means a lot to me." After giving a slight glance at Karthik, Krithi said this to Devyani and then moved to Karthik, saying, "Take care of yourself and get back soon I'll be in touch with you.. Sorry for everything."

Krithi and Karthik's eyes were filled with tears. Govind, noticing this, was confused and asked Radhika why they were so emotional. Radhika explained, "Karthik proposed to Krithi, but she didn't accept because she didn't want to disturb her studies. That's why I'm proud of my sister," Govind said. "But Krithi also liked him. She just didn't express it, and that's why her eyes are filled with tears. She's not only missing us, but she's also missing someone she loves and doesn't know if he can wait for her."

Govind continued, "Oh, I see. Now I understand. When I think about our moments from these three days, I can sense it about Karthik. He is deeply in love with her and will do anything for her. That's how we met as well. He is the reason for the togetherness of our family. We can talk to both Karthik and Krithi once her studies are completed. Don't worry about it."

Krithi said goodbye to everyone and headed to the airport for check-in. The others waited, watching until Krithi disappeared from sight. Once she was out of view, Govind turned to Karthik and, with a smile, said, "Hey, brother-in-law, I'm so happy for you, dear. Don't worry, she will come back." Govind placed his hand on Karthik's shoulder, offering him reassurance and support.

After that, Govind and Karthik departed together, heading to Karthik's home. Govind could see how much Karthik cared for Krithi, and although the situation was emotional, he believed that Krithi and Karthik would eventually find their way back to each other once the time was right.

After reaching Karthik's home, they all had dinner. Then, Krithi called her father and informed him that she had checked in and was waiting for boarding. Next, she called Karthik's mom and told her the same. Finally, she called Karthik.

Karthik answered without even saying hello. "Miss you, Krithi," he said.

She took a deep breath. "It took two days to hear my name from you. Don't be like this, Karthik, please. I feel dull when you do, and I won't be able to focus on my studies. Please, be like a family member to me," Krithi pleaded.

"Hmm... okay," Karthik responded.

"Did you eat anything?" he asked.

"No, I'm looking for some juice. We can get food on the flight," she replied.

"Okay, drink some juice and take care. Call me once you land. Get a SIM card as soon as possible. I'll wait for you, Krithi," Karthik said.

"Karthikkk, please... bye, take care," Krithi said before ending the call.

A few days passed, and both Karthik's family and Krithi's family grew closer. One day, Karthik's mother expressed her wish for Karthik and Krithi to get married once Krithi completed her studies. Krithi's family happily welcomed the proposal, feeling it was a great match. However, for Krithi, this news remained a silent suspense in her heart.

As days went by, everyone got busy with their own responsibilities. Krithi focused on her studies and adjusting to her new environment, while Karthik worked hard to complete his projects as quickly as possible. Life seemed to be moving forward smoothly—until one day, everything turned upside down.

Out of nowhere, the police arrived at Karthik's home. The sound of their sirens and the sudden knock on the door sent chills down his family's spine. When Karthik's father opened the door, he was stunned to see police officers standing there with a warrant.

"We are here to arrest Karthik," one of the officers announced.

Karthik and his parents froze in shock. His mother clutched her saree tightly, her face turning pale. His father, struggling to process the situation, asked, "What do you mean? What has my son done?"

"He is involved in a cybercrime," the officer stated firmly, holding up the arrest warrant.

Karthik's mind went blank. Cybercrime? What were they talking about? He had never done anything illegal.

"There must be some mistake," his father protested. "My son is not involved in any crime!"

But the police didn't listen. They took Karthik into custody, ignoring the cries of his mother and the desperate pleas of his father.

The shocking news spread like wildfire. The accusation was linked to Karthik's office—someone had committed fraud using his system. But the police had no solid proof yet, only an allegation. Karthik had no idea how this had happened, yet he was the one being dragged into a nightmare he never saw coming.

The next day, Krithi's family heard about Karthik's arrest. The moment the news reached them, Krithi's father was furious.

"I will not allow my daughter to marry a criminal!" he declared. Without a second thought, he decided to break off the proposal.

However, Radhika, Krithi's mother, refused to jump to conclusions. "We don't even know the truth yet," she reasoned. "Let's wait until the court gives its verdict."

"No! My decision is final," Krithi's father insisted. "I will not let Krithi's future be ruined because of this scandal."

As days passed, he even began searching for a new match for Krithi, determined to marry her off to someone else. But Krithi was devastated. She rejected every proposal that came her way, unable to think of anyone else but Karthik. She worried about him day and night, praying for his innocence to be proven.

One day, unable to bear the pressure any longer, she finally gathered the courage to speak up.

"I love Karthik," she confessed to her father, her voice trembling. "I don't care what the world says. I know he is innocent."

Her father's anger flared. "Enough, Krithi! How can you still say that after what happened? He is accused of a crime!"

"I believe in him," she insisted. "And I won't marry anyone else."

A few days later, Krithi's father's close friend, Narayan a police officer, visited their home. During their conversation, Krithi's father couldn't hide his frustration.

"I don't understand this girl," he vented. "Even after Karthik's arrest, she still wants to marry him! How can I let my daughter ruin her life?"

Narayan listened carefully. "Show me Karthik's photo," he said.

Curious but skeptical, Krithi's father handed him a picture of Karthik. Narayan stared at it for a long moment before his expression changed.

"This case... I'm the one handling it," he revealed.

Krithi's father was stunned. "What?"

"Yes. But Karthik hasn't been confirmed as guilty yet. It's just an allegation," Narayan explained. "In fact, I've been investigating this case myself, and I have a feeling he's not the culprit. But I can't be certain yet. These days, even the most innocent-looking people can be involved in crimes."

At that moment, another person stepped forward—Govind, Krithi's cousin, who had also been quietly listening.

"Daddy, I'm also tracking this case but I'm not dealing with it," Govind said. "And I know Karthik isn't that kind of person. We should wait before making any decisions."

Krithi's father still looked doubtful, but Govind continued, "Do you have any evidence against him?"

Narayan nodded. "We have some office security camera footage."

"Can I see it?" Govind asked.

Narayan hesitated for a moment, then nodded. "I'll arrange it."

Radhika told entire Narayan uncle conversation to Kirthi, For the first time, hope flickered in Krithi's heart. If there was proof, then maybe—just maybe—they could find out the real truth behind the scam.

Narayan arranged CCTV footage for Govind but insisted that he work with their team before accessing the videos. To facilitate this, Narayan requested the officials to grant Govind permission, as he was working in the CID department. Once the team was formed, Govind joined Narayan and started the investigation.

On March 25, while reviewing the footage, they found a suspicious video where an unknown person was using Karthik's system. Govind enquired in the office about who had used Karthik's system, and Office boy said it's Prasad and he wore same shirt that day isn't in he asked employees there to reconfirm then identified the person in the video as Prasad.

The police brought Prasad in for questioning. When confronted, Prasad admitted, "Yes, I used Karthik's system to access a file when he was on leave. I asked him for his password, shared the file, and logged out. But I don't know how anything illegal happened. I did nothing wrong."

The police applied pressure to get the truth from Prasad, using various interrogation techniques. Prasad, frustrated, said, **"If you scare me and force me to confess, you might get an answer, but not the truth."**

Realizing that intimidation was ineffective, the police used a polygraph test, which confirmed that Prasad was telling the truth. The officers then asked him to cooperate with the investigation and share any suspicions he had about his colleagues. Prasad insisted that everyone in the office was dedicated to their work and denied any knowledge of wrongdoing. He was then released.

With the case still unsolved, Govind decided to analyze more footage from the days Karthik was absent. After carefully reviewing the videos, he noticed something unusual—someone resembling Prasad had used the system. However, upon zooming in on the screen's reflection, Govind saw another face, though it was not entirely clear. He then suggested creating a sketch based on the visible features.

A sketch artist was called in, and a facial sketch was prepared. Govind, Narayan, and their team took the sketch to Karthik's office and showed it to the manager and Prasad. Both were shocked to recognize the person—it was the office boy who delivered coffee to Prasad while he was using Karthik's system.

Prasad then recalled, "Yes! He came that day and gave me coffee, even though I didn't ask for it. But we never thought he had any computer knowledge; we assumed he was uneducated."

The police took the office boy into custody and interrogated him for several hours. Eventually, he confessed to the crime. He admitted that he had planned the scam for a long time and deliberately joined the company as an office boy a month ago to execute it.

With the truth revealed, Karthik was cleared of suspicion. Everyone was relieved that the real culprit had been caught, and justice was served.

After a long year of struggle, investigation, and court hearings, Karthik was finally proven innocent. The real culprit was caught, and Karthik came out of the case without any criminal record. He was declared genuine, and all allegations against him were dropped.

One day, Krithi's father called Karthik.

“Karthik... I owe you an apology,” he said sincerely. “After a month, Krithi will complete her MS degree. Your aunt and I are traveling to attend Krithi's convocation. Would you like to join us?”

“Yes, Uncle, I'd love to. But I want to meet her in India, Uncle. I want those reunion vibes in India. After hearing everything from Radhika Bhabhi and Govind about what Krithi went through because of the allegations against me—how she suffered yet still trusted me unwaveringly—I feel that our meeting should happen in India. I want that moment to be special, where I can look into her eyes and assure her that everything is fine now. I'll come to the airport, but please don't tell Krithi. Act like you're still furious with me—I want to surprise her."

Her father chuckled. "Alright, Karthik. As you wish."

On the day of the convocation, after the ceremony, Krithi and her parents went for dinner. That same day, Krithi's father asked her about marriage. "I have selected a guy for you, dear. When will you get married?"

Krithi insisted, "Daddy, I already told you that I love Karthik. Please don't think of anyone else for me."

Her father became furious. "Why do you like him? He just came out of jail! Why do you still want him?" he asked angrily.

Krithi replied, "Daddy, he was proven innocent. All the allegations were false—that's why he was released. Why don't you understand this? Please, Daddy, I want him."

"No, Krithi! You have to marry the man I chose for you. He will come to Hyderabad once we land, and that's final. You have to meet him in Hyderabad," her father declared.

Krithi firmly responded, "If you don't accept Karthik, then I won't marry anyone. Even if Karthik marries someone else, I will remain single."

Krithi's father and mother observed how deeply Krithi loved Karthik. Everyone became silent, and they finished their dinner. They returned to their hotel for the night. The next day, they vacated the hotel and flew back to India.

Krithi was coming back with a heavy heart. If Karthik met her, what would she say? She knew he would become emotional if she told him her father was not accepting their love.

Finally, after a long and exhausting journey, Krithi and her parents landed in India. The moment they stepped off the plane, Krithi felt a mix of emotions—relief, nervousness, and anticipation. They collected their luggage and slowly walked towards the airport exit. As the doors slid open, they saw a familiar group of people waiting for them.

Radhika, Govind, Seethu, Devyani, and Rajiv stood with bright smiles, eagerly waving at them. Seeing their warm faces, Krithi couldn't help but smile back. She quickened her pace, her heart pounding, but her eyes kept searching for someone—Karthik. She scanned the crowd, hoping to see him, but he was nowhere in sight. A slight disappointment flickered across her face, but she quickly masked it with a smile as she reached her loved ones.

The moment Krithi saw Seethu, she couldn't control her emotions. She ran to her, hugged her tightly, and even lifted her up in excitement, showing just how much she had missed her. "Seethu! I missed you so much!" she said, her voice filled with joy. Radhika chuckled and gently took Krithi's handbag from her, while the others helped carry the rest of the luggage. As they all moved a little further, chatting excitedly, something unexpected happened.

Just then, from the corner of her eye, Krithi noticed a familiar figure stepping forward. Her breath caught in her throat as she turned to see Karthik standing right in front of her. Time seemed to freeze. Her eyes widened in disbelief, and her heart raced. She had imagined this moment a thousand times, but now that it was happening, she was overwhelmed. Tears welled up in her eyes as Karthik walked towards her, his gaze fixed on hers. Without a word, he gently took her hands in his.

With a warm smile, Karthik slowly got down on one knee, holding a small velvet box in his hand. As he opened it, a beautiful ring sparkled inside.

"Krithi, I've waited so long for this moment. Through every hardship, every struggle, you stood by me. You never stopped believing in me, even when the world did. Today, I want to promise you that I will always stand by you, just like you did for me. Will you marry me?"

Tears streamed down Krithi's face as she looked at him, unable to speak. The man she loved, the man she had fought for, was here, asking her to be his forever. It felt like a dream come true.

Just then, a loud voice interrupted the moment.

"Krithiiiii! That's the guy I chose for you, isn't it?"

It was her father, shouting from a distance, looking towards Karthik's parents. His tone carried a mix of pride and realization. For a moment, everyone turned towards him, stunned. Then, slowly, a smile formed on Krithi's lips. She turned back to Karthik, her heart bursting with love and happiness.

With a trembling hand, she reached out, took the ring from him, and whispered, "Yes, Karthik. A thousand times, yes."

Karthik smiled as he slipped the ring onto her finger, sealing their promise. As soon as he did, Krithi threw her arms around him, holding him tightly. The entire airport echoed with applause and cheers from their families and friends.

Both families embraced and celebrated the long-awaited union, finally accepting their love wholeheartedly. In that moment, all the struggles, all the pain, and all the waiting felt worth it. Soon, Karthik and Krithi would be married, their love story forever sealed in a bond that no one could break.

After spending some time together, everyone went to Karthik's home. Krithi, feeling a bit tired from the journey, took some rest. That evening, she and Karthik decided to revisit the coffee shop where they had their first coffee together during her shopping trip. Sitting at the same spot, they reminisced about that special day, cherishing the beautiful memories they had created.

After enjoying their coffee and taking a short ride around the city, they went out for dinner. The evening was peaceful and filled with love as they walked hand in hand, growing closer with each step. They talked about their journey together, their future, and the excitement that lay ahead.

Karthik turned to Krithi and said, "Krithi, today my place looks even more beautiful because I'm with you. Wherever we go, it feels more beautiful, even though I've grown up here. Thank you for coming into my life." He held her hand, and every moment felt special as they shared laughter and deep conversations.

Karthik tried to tease her and adjusted his voice, saying, "No, no, all thanks to my love, Seethu, the cute girl. She is the reason I can see even the most ordinary places as beautiful and feel peace in my heartIt's because of her that we met. I still remember our sweet memories from Devyani's wedding and the trip."

Krithi chuckled and playfully replied, "Oh, is it? Just now, you said I'm the reason you can see regular places even more beautiful?"

The next day, Krithi and her family returned to their home in Visakhapatnam, while Karthik got back to his busy work schedule. Despite the distance, they made sure to meet every weekend—either Krithi would visit Karthik, or he would travel to see her. Their love grew stronger with each meeting, and they eagerly looked forward to the day they would finally be together forever.

After a few days, both families came together to discuss and finalize the wedding date. Following tradition, they matched the couple's astral charts and made all the necessary arrangements with great joy and excitement. From selecting the wedding venue to planning every little detail, the preparations were done with love and care, ensuring that their big day would be nothing short of perfect.

The much-awaited wedding day arrived, and the air was filled with excitement and joy. The ceremony took place in a beautiful, traditional Andhra setting, with colorful flowers adorning the venue and the fragrance of jasmine filling the air. The bride, Krithi, was a vision of grace in her vibrant red handloom silk saree, with intricate gold jewelry and her hair adorned with fresh flowers. Her eyes sparkled with happiness as she sat in front of the decorated mandap, surrounded by family members and friends, all eagerly waiting for the sacred rituals to begin.

As the priest began the rituals, Karthik stood by Krithi's side, wearing a crisp white dhoti and a traditional white shirt. His heart raced as he looked at her, feeling the weight of this special moment. The couple exchanged sweet glances, with the entire ceremony echoing the blessings of their loved ones. The atmosphere was filled with sacred chants as the couple moved forward to tie the *mangal sutra* around Krithi's neck, symbolizing their eternal bond. This moment marked the true beginning of their married life, and

Krithi's eyes shone with emotion as Karthik carefully tied the sacred thread, signifying their commitment to one another.

After the *mangal sutra* was tied, the couple exchanged garlands in the *Jaimala* ceremony. They exchanged the beautiful floral garlands, signifying their mutual acceptance and respect. Krithi's face lit up with a radiant smile as she placed the garland around Karthik's neck, marking the continuation of their journey together. The entire family cheered as they exchanged heartfelt vows, with tears of joy glistening in Krithi's eyes. The wedding ceremony concluded with blessings from the elders, and the couple was showered with flower petals, symbolizing the purity and beauty of their love. The day was filled with love, laughter, and a sense of unity as Krithi and Karthik embarked on their new journey as husband and wife.

After their special day filled with traditional rituals and fun games, Karthik and Krithi finally made their way to a colorful, fragrant room where they could have the privacy they deserved. Both sat together, and Karthik looked at Krithi, his voice soft and sincere.

"Krithi," he began, "we've shared so much with each other, from the moment we met to now, but today, I want to share something more."

Krithi looked at him, intrigued, as Karthik gently asked, "Could you sit properly so I can lie down in your lap? I want to feel close to you."

Krithi, understanding his request, smiled softly and adjusted herself so that Karthik could rest his head in her lap. She asked him to lay down, and as he did, he held her hand, his voice filled with emotion. "Krithi, we've shared so many things in our conversations, but today, I need to share something deeper with you."

He continued, his words heavy with emotion, "As you know, when I went through the scam case, I faced things I can't explain to anyone. The torture and humiliation were unbearable. My confidence was crushed. But then, I remembered you. I had to stay strong, stay confident. I had to clear my name, because only then could I be with you. And as soon as I got out of it, all I wanted was to come to the USA and meet you. I thought, if you're with me, I can face anything. Krithi, I can face everything with you... you're my strength. I love you."

Krithi listened intently, her heart aching. "Karthik, you don't know how much pain I felt during that time," she said, her voice trembling. "My dad even said there was no chance for us, but I never lost hope in you. I knew you'd come back. I could feel your suffering, not just because of the case, but for me too. I felt your pain in my heart, and it hurt so much. But after all the struggles, we're finally here now."

Karthik smiled softly, feeling at peace. "Yes, finally, I'm in your lap, my kind of heaven."

Krithi leaned down and kissed his forehead, their first kiss. Karthik, deeply moved by the moment, woke from his thoughts, pulled her into a tight embrace, and held her close.

And as the night continued, their love for each other only grew stronger.

In the end, their journey was not just about overcoming obstacles, but about finding a love so deep and unwavering that it made everything else fade away—together, they had everything they needed to face the world.

Thank You!

Kinnera Venkat

Gmail: Kinnera095@gmail.com

www.ingramcontent.com/pod-product-compliance
Lightning Source LLC
LaVergne TN
LVHW040905150826
845672LV00007B/1900

* 9 7 9 8 8 9 7 4 4 4 7 8 6 *